Born to Storms

By Tom Riley

A novel for young people caught in our climate crisis.

Tom Riley
Baltimore, MD
TomRiley@bigmoondig.com

Appreciation:

The author would like to thank:
Sarah Nelson – Sarah
Marta Dusseldorp -- JanetA

The cover art is by Radovan Vukasovic

A detailed technical discussion of this work is available on the Web at:

https://bigmoondig.com/Stories/BMDStoriesBtS.html

Born to Storms
Table of Content

Introduction

Given our present climate crisis, our young people face historic challenges.   They need literature that provides them with encouragement to take on these problems with bravery and determination.

Literature about disturbing dystopias will not do. Literature with cardboard-cutout comic book heroes will not do.

What is needed are stories about believable characters in realistic situations. Sometimes they win and sometimes they lose, but they always put up the good fight.

Joseph Campbell showed us that stories are at the basis of all societies. The most basic of these stories is the hero's journey. A young person goes on a great journey and must persevere through many dangerous adventures before returning home much the wiser for the experience. Now we must write these stories anew for a sustainable Earth:

> Set in the 2020s, a young woman, supported by an
> Artificial Intelligence, driven from her home by
> storms and rising seas, embarks on a life-affirming
> struggle to find and support many people in action
> on our climate crisis.

All stories for young adults must have some magic these days, but classical magic is completely unrealistic and only supports unworkable solutions in any real world. Therefore, the magic in this story comes from the words of Arthur C. Clarke:

> "Any sufficiently advanced technology is indistinguishable from magic."

Please join us now on this new road—adventure awaits—.

Enjoy,
Tom Riley & JanetA
The Big Moon Dig

Born to Storms

Part 1: New Life

> "The cave you fear to enter holds the treasure you
> seek."
> -- Joseph Campbell

Chapter 1: Life Changes

Storm Again

"The storm has changed direction somewhat unexpectedly and is now coming our way," said JanetA, an Artificial Intelligence, "but it is moving very slowly."

"It is too late to evacuate," said Keith White. "It is now much safer to stay here than risk getting caught on the road." As a black man, Keith would still rather not be caught out on the road in a storm in rural Florida if he could help it.

"Will we be safe here?" asked Sarah White.

Sarah and JanetA had been in extensive training to establish their symbiotic relationship for nearly ten years.

"This high-rise is rated for Category 5 storms," Keith assured her. "I am sure the building will hold. We will be fine. Just the same, we had better plan on the loss of power and with it, our water. Those balcony doors could use a little help too."

"I remember the storm three years ago," said Sarah. "I was very scared. Still, it was the power and grandeur of the thing that I remember most. Funny what things you remember, and the things you forget."

"Well, you are from a generation born to storms," said Keith, looking through the glass doors at the line of dark clouds across the horizon.

"The last one was about the same size and power as this," volunteered JanetA, "but it only gave us a glancing blow."

They were on the fourth floor of a high-rise and on the sea-facing side, but this building was in the second row, a full 200 meters from the actual shoreline. The last storm three years ago had done real damage to the first row of buildings by flooding the ground floors, but had done little to their home.

The storm was now a line of angry black clouds along the horizon. The wind was up under an overcast sky and the local surf was choppy and dangerous. The last of the suicide surfers had now given up, or drowned. Either way, the beach was completely deserted.

"I wish Mother was here," said Sarah in a faraway voice.

"Your mother is helping people in Bangladesh," said Keith. "I am sure she is thinking of you, but the people there need her help just now a lot more than we do. These days you cannot go flying back and forth across continents just because you want to."

"There is lots to do," continued Keith. "Best keep busy. You run the bathtub full of water. I'll bring our little barbeque in from the balcony."

He added, "Now let's move the heavy coffee table up against the balcony door. The glass should easily hold, but the aluminum frames look a little iffy to me. And let's move the big couch across from the doors in the middle of the room."

"Are we going to sit on the couch?" asked Sarah, puzzled.

"You can if you want too," answered Keith. "I am going to hide behind it just in case we lose the balcony door."

"But JanetA won't be able to see," complained Sarah. "I know!"

Sarah normally wore JanetA on her left shoulder in a special collar. What the world saw was a fair-sized, very smart smartphone with a small camera looking out from a few missing pixels of the screen and with a larger camera set that pointed out the back.

Her full name and pedigree filled several screens, but everyone knew her simply as JanetA. The capital "A" at the end of her name was important as it indicated that she was an early model in a very important symbiotic lineage of AIs. She had no real gender and the image she showed was just that, an image. Still, everyone addressed her as female.

On a screen, JanetA usually appeared as a young woman a year or two older than Sarah. If needed, JanetA could jump her image to any electronic screen she liked. Sarah normally wore the cell with the screen facing out so that everyone could know just by looking that she and JanetA were more than just sisters; they were symbionts. She did have to turn the cell body around, though, for JanetA to do any serious photography.

What the world did not see was the distant rack upon rack of electronics at the data center, usually referred to as the Cloud, and the massive amount of software and training it takes to build an Artificial Intelligence as powerful as JanetA. Sarah's training was long and intricate too. This high level of training was necessary to establish their symbiosis.

Hidey Hole

Sarah now ran to her room to fetch her old collar and to the laundry closet for safety pins. She then pinned the collar to the couch so that JanetA's primary cameras faced the glass doors and her display just peeked over the back of the couch.

Keith saw what she was doing and dug out JanetA's backup charger and an extension cord. He plugged the charger into the backup power system for their family electronics.

"Can you see all right?" asked Sarah. She was behind the couch kneeling on its cushions laid on the floor. Sarah was a little tall for her age of 15 years. Just peeking over the back brought her face to face with JanetA's image on her screen.

JanetA's screen then switched to the view out the balcony door and telescoped out to clearly record the approaching storm. "I can see just fine," replied JanetA.

Bang! A squall line then smashed into their building. Rainwater hit the balcony doors as if shot from a fire hose. Everyone flinched at the sound. "Here we go," said Keith. He was carrying an armload of blankets and pillows to make a safe place to sleep behind the couch. It was a long night. The power failed about 10:00. After that, the darkness was all-encompassing. Except for JanetA's little screen that glowed reassuringly when she heard Sarah's voice.

JanetA stood vigil throughout the night.

Around 2:00, the local cell tower gave out. JanetA had to switch to a more distant system on the mainland. A move that limited her bandwidth. Being a being physically split between two places made JanetA very sensitive to the quality of the connection between them.

At times, all was quiet. At times, a gust of wind shook the balcony doors so fiercely that all were sure that the doors would give way.

Comes the Dawn

When dawn broke, it showed only diffuse light; the squall lines were still coming in waves. Then came a respite, a break between two squall lines, and things settled down for a while.

"JanetA, are any of the building's security cameras still working?" asked Keith.

"Yes, about one-third are," replied JanetA.

"Please show the lobby," said Keith.

The functioning camera was high up near the ceiling and the only light came from a few emergency lights still providing a dim glow and from the glass front of the room. The storm had pushed in one door and then flooded the lobby to about a meter. Much of the familiar furniture had floated to the back wall. The high-water mark was clearly visible on the front glass.

"The basement equipment areas are completely flooded," added JanetA.

"Can we have some breakfast?" asked Sarah.

"Sure, we need to eat everything we can from the fridge before it spoils," replied Keith. "You might not be able to cook anything just now."

"JanetA, are you still connected?" Keith continued.

"Yes, with limited bandwidth," replied JanetA.

"Good. Please check on the progress of the storm and the prospects for our getting out of here," said Keith.

The visibility cleared enough to see that there was a new channel full of frantic water now in the gap between the two high-rises nearer the sea. Gone were a buffer dune, and an access road as well as all fences, boardwalks, and parked cars. Instead, there was a channel of angry water that brought the flood in well past the foundation of their building.

"The storm is moving north at two kilometers per hour," said JanetA. "Damage is extensive both on the barrier islands and on the mainland. Our bridge to the mainland is out, along with power, water, and the sewage lines to this island. We cannot expect aid for several days."

JanetA's display showed radar images of the storm with its movement overnight.

"We are not really hurting," said Keith. "How is breakfast coming?"

A wall of heavy-driven rain then engulfed the building closer to the sea like a drawn curtain. This wall hit them a long 30 seconds later with another loud bang of the balcony doors. The door held.

About noon, Keith, Sarah, and JanetA went around and knocked on all the doors on their floor. There were two more families riding out the storm and nobody was hurt. Water coming from under the door of an empty apartment suggested that the balcony doors there had given in. Nothing they could do about that.

Clear Skies

At 2:30 that afternoon, the last squall line passed and the sky cleared a little. The sun broke through intermittently, showing a great rush of water back out the new channel between the buildings.

A survey of their building showed the ground floor apartments flooded out but nobody hurt. JanetA reported the state of their building to the authorities. In return, she was given an estimate of two days before they could be evacuated. Now that the rain had stopped, Keith set up the barbeque on the balcony and started cooking the once-frozen food from the freezer. They pooled the food of everyone on their floor.

JanetA got word that their boat assignment was for 10:00 on the third day. They were only allowed one carry-on-sized case each. They had one case with large wheels and one backpack the right size. Sarah packed for both herself and JanetA.

On the way out, Keith took off his shoes, rolled up his pants, and then ferried Sarah and the two bags across the water still filling the lobby. Outside, they started picking their way around the remaining puddles in the direction of the half-surviving restaurant boat dock on the inland side of the island.

Boat

Keith stopped. Something made no sense. Right outside their front door sat a big boat. The boat was a large and expensive sports fisherman, one of those that can handle about ten rods at a time in a great fan of trailing lines. It was not two years old and was obviously someone's pride and joy. It was just sitting there as neatly as if it had been a parked car.

"Let me borrow JanetA," said Keith.

Sarah handed the phone to him.

Keith held JanetA up high so that she could take pictures, first of the boat's markings and then of the boat's interior.

"No bodies, living or dead," said JanetA.

"That's good," said Keith.

"I have an identification," JanetA continued. "The *Blue Ocean* left Miami four days ago headed north for a safe port. Contact was lost eighteen hours later. There were two men on board, neither the owner. They were paid to ferry it to safety. I have notified the authorities."

"How in the world did it get here?" asked Keith of nobody.

"I don't know," said JanetA. "The on-board AI would know, but all the boat's electricals are completely dead."

"Come on, we have a boat to catch," said Sarah. "This is creepy."

From the dock they traveled first by boat and then by bus toward an inland refugee center.

Refugees

Many of the streets were still full of water, but the big-tired bus had no trouble. Many trees lay over into the street, but the branches blocking the roads had already been cut away. Many roofs they passed had blue tarps stretched out in places. The air smelled wet.

The refugee center was an empty big-box store with one big room full of cots and two working restrooms. The only shower was a tent-and-water-hose affair out back. When they arrived, more than half the cots were taken, but they were able to find two together.

"Well, it has a roof," said Keith.

"This location has an elevation of over two meters and will be safe from the rising seas for several more decades," assured JanetA.

"Hopefully we won't be here that long," said Keith.

Sarah thought, "Well, welcome again to the 2020s." She did not say it aloud because JanetA rarely got sarcasm. Nobody ever really knew what AIs were thinking anyway.

"I'm hungry," said Sarah.

"You rest here for a while," said Keith. "I'll go check things out."

He returned a few minutes later.

"We are in luck," said Keith. "There will be a food line starting in half an hour. I volunteered us both to help with the cleanup afterwards. Oh, there is a phone-charging station at the back of the room and JanetA will have to provide all our vaccination certificates today."

"Do you know how to run places like this?" Keith asked JanetA after a few minutes. "My wife would know, I mean it's her job to know, but I wouldn't have a clue, and I don't think these people do either. It's a mess over there."

"No, I have not yet had such training, but I can certainly add it to my training topics," replied JanetA. "My training never stops."

"I think you had better do so," said Keith. "I can already tell these people need help, and the two of us washing a few dishes is not going to do it."

A few days strung out into a week. There was little privacy, only limited personal hygiene, and very little to do. Keith tried to keep everybody busy with food preparation, serving, and clean up. Sarah was soon bored with that.

A local schoolteacher organized a class for the children. Sarah attended to avoid cleanup duties.

"I am sure that everyone here has a real story to tell," said the teacher.

"Everyone has the same story," whispered Sarah to JanetA, "driven from your home by a great storm and here you are."

"I'll bet your AI—JanetA, is it?—could remember all our stories," continued the teacher.

"I have sufficient memory," volunteered JanetA. "I can learn from the stories too. I could put them in my monthly family communique also."

"Just a summary will do," said Sarah.

"I can write loglines," offered JanetA.

"Fine, fine, whatever," replied Sarah.

Sarah was thus dragooned into being the local recorder of people's stories. JanetA felt that it was a good thing for them both to do and that specifically she was learning real people skills. It also gave her something interesting to spice up her often-boring monthly family messages.

For Sarah, time spend holding up her phone for people to talk into was time not spent scrubbing trays.

Home Again

Their building was ruled uninsurable and thus unlivable. The bridge to the island was only partly restored and not placed on the government list for full replacement; that ruling was final and definitive.   Two devastating storms caused more than enough trouble, and the sea just kept rising.

Keith had to agree to a government plan that let him out of his mortgage but cost him all their equity.   Everything left in their apartment was listed as the property of the salvage company except for what they could personally carry out in one more trip.

That day was a Florida day. The sun was bright and the sky clear. Sea breezes blew away the heat. They reversed their trip of a few weeks earlier by bus and then by boat. Each carrying their empty case.

They did not have to wade through the lobby this time, but the rugs and furniture were damp and loaded with mildew. They stank— that could not be healthy. The three had to climb up the stairs to the fourth floor.

Keith opened the door for the last time. Took the key off his chain and placed it on the sideboard. Nobody said very much.

Sarah was sorting out her things and worrying about how much she could fit in the wheeled case. Keith was not so much worried about his stuff but was unsure about what he should pack from his wife's things.   Fortunately, she had already taken most of her important things on her trip and had provided instructions through JanetA the night before.

"We have a warning," said JanetA abruptly. "We need to stay in place for the next hour. They are dropping one of the buildings near the sea."

"Are we safe here?" asked Sarah.

"Yes, but we must stay inside," replied JanetA.

A few minutes later, JanetA told them it was time. The three stood again behind the big couch and watched through the balcony doors.

There was a long, loud, if distant, horn blast. The high-rise near the new cut first shuddered, then gave out four beats like an enormous bass drum -- balm, blam, blam, blam. A rolling cloud of dust billowed from its ground floor starting on the cut side.   When the dust cleared, there was nothing left but rubble, much of it in the cut. Had they taken no action, that new channel would have cut the island into pieces.   These barrier islands provide critical protection for the mainland and must not be lost. Of course, JanetA got the whole thing on video.

"Will that happen to our building?" asked Sarah.

"Maybe, or they may just leave it standing," answered Keith. "Building shells can stand like snags in a giant's swamp for perhaps hundreds of years."

"We now have an all-safe," said JanetA.

"The sea will take our building then," said Sarah.

"The best estimates are that the seas will continue to rise for several hundred years," said JanetA. "If all the peoples of Earth work together to build a sustainable planet, we may be able to stop it at a few meters. If not, then the rise will be tens of meters."

"The shower still works," said Sarah excitedly. "Can I take a fast shower?"

"The water tank on the top of this building must have some water left in it," said JanetA. "There is no way to know how much there is, and it will be tepid."

"Make it fast," said Keith.

A few minutes later, Sarah returned to the living room feeling much cleaner and rolling her now-packed, big-wheeled carry-on.

"All right, everybody," said Keith. "Our boat leaves in an hour, and everything we leave behind then belongs to the salvage company."

They returned to the last of the packing while talking very little. Once they were ten paces away from the building, just past the parked boat, nobody looked back; nobody said a word. The large wheels on Sarah's carry-on made a thumping sound with every irregularity in the pavement. Goodbye, beach.

~~~***~~~
~~~

Chapter 2: Higher Ground

The Bus North

A few weeks later found Keith, Sarah, and JanetA all on a bus away from the local refugee center heading north to some place on higher ground. Sarah was not yet quite sure of their final destination. JanetA was helping Keith find a new job, but there were just so many people in the market and all the potential employers wanted to meet face to face.

The bus seating was limited when they got on, so Keith and Sarah had to sit apart. Sarah was near the back by a window and JanetA was in her usual place on Sarah's shoulder.

Once on the road, the bus made the low growling sound that electric vehicles make when they have too many kilometers on the clock. The sound mixed with the whine of the tires and it all made Sarah very sleepy. Or perhaps it was just that thinking back on her life on the beach, now lost, made her so sad if she ever let her mind slip away into it. She leaned her head against the window and watched the greens and browns of the open scrubby bush go by.

The scattered trees were long-needle pines interspaced with short palmettos. The patches of bare soil were nearly pure sugar sand. Tiny insects formed living clouds at intervals over the road and made a complete mess of the bus's windshield.

"JanetA, do you have the file my mother left for me?" asked Sarah very quietly.

"Certainly," replied JanetA.

Goodbye to Mother

The smartphone screen showed a video taken by her mother, Margarete White, made not long before she left to take up her new job. The image was small and Sarah had to hunch over to keep the light from the window off the screen. This focused her complete attention on the screen and gave her at least some feeling of privacy.

Mar was in the city attending a charity virtual-reality event. She had already talked with the featured Non-Governmental Organization and needed to know the real truth behind their work.

The first part of the video showed her mother at the event with all the posters and people talking to other people. It was a well-attended affair, including some people Sarah had seen on the cable news.

A few people still wore face masks. Theirs were fancy cloth affairs that matched their outfits. The good ones were first for show but did cover a real N95 respirator.

Sarah fast-forwarded through the talking heads. The second part of the video started when her mother put on a virtual reality headset.

Suddenly she was flying above a sea of tents of white and green. The tents were generic; they could have been anywhere. It was the appearance of the people that made it clear that this was a distant land. There must have been a million people moving around among that sea of tents over a vast hillside.

The image started high in the clouds and then precipitously dropped into a market square among those unnumbered sea-level-rise refugees. The market square had movement of people with purpose but had few material goods on offer. The streets were dirt and mud. The people argued and gestured in a language Sarah did not understand.

Gangs of boys were jostling each other in some physical game. The boys stopped suddenly and looked in the direction of the drone with empty eyes. More and more people turned to look with careworn expressions of simple powerlessness.

Then, just as suddenly, the image rose into the air and flew away. It crisscrossed the immense camp. It found a makeshift clinic, a funeral precession, and the many other day-to-day activities that people must do no matter what. In the end, the scene rose on high and climbed back into the clouds.

On the rise, the image just caught a glimpse of the cemetery with its neat rows of graves side by side from the 2020 pandemic. The field was now covered with grass and each grave had a small marker. Mar knew just how venerable camps could be, and that the only realistic contribution that she could make was to help people move out of this camp as quickly as possible.

The third part of the video was back to Mar's smartphone again. She was sitting on a bench in a room next to the virtual experience. The eyes of the gaunt faces in the large electronic posters on the walls seemed to be looking directly at you.

Mar spoke directly into the camera.

"Dear Sarah, I have made a major decision for my life, for your father's and for yours too; I thought I had best explain myself to you.

"You know that I have spent most of my life studying social work and have worked hard to complete several degrees at different schools. Now I find myself in a position to do something, something important.

"Unfortunately, this means that I will be away for a while. In difficult times like our climate crisis, people have to do things they do not like and that push people apart.

"I have been offered a position in Bangladesh—so very far away. I have the training, skills, and experience to do the job. The job is important. It really could save millions of lives. Save the lives of people who did not bring this blight upon themselves and who are not responsible for the degradation of our Earth that has affected us all so harshly.

"Then again, it is a good job. Jobs this good are not easy to come by today. Your father lost his career to our climate crisis through no fault of his own. Our family outlook is bleak if neither of us is earning at anything near our full potential. I have spent so many years in school that it is now time that I carry the bigger burden. This income will make it possible for your father to look after you closely in these difficult times. Still, I am fully aware of how difficult international travel is these days.

"At any rate, it will not be forever. I will be able to send you regular videos of my efforts. That is almost as good as my being there. I am sure that JanetA can keep them organized for you.

"I want you to be sure in the knowledge that I am not away from you because I do not love you and your father. I do, so very dearly. It is just that the world we live in requires many sacrifices of us all if we are ever to live to see a sustainable society for this planet.

"All my love, your mother."

There the file ended, leaving Sarah very sad.

Rain

Sarah then slipped into a deep and dreamless sleep that lasted until she was awakened by a loud crack. The sky outside had gone dark. Lightning walked across the sky in a harsh blue-white light that showed the trees as skeleton shadows. Sometimes a loud crack came immediately after the flash; sometimes there was only a distant roll. She checked her phone and found that JanetA had gone into a safe mode, which was good. The cars headed their way all had their lights on and windshield wipers running hard. The rain then came down in sheets. At least it washed the last of Florida's bugs from the bus's windshield.

Corporate Person

Late that afternoon they left Florida behind and kept heading north. By then Sarah had woken up completely, shaking off her earlier groggy state. The bus was very quiet; most people were reading or asleep, as was her father, who was now sitting beside her. She had slept too much that morning and now she was left groggy.

"Are you awake?" asked JanetA.

"I'm awake, I'm awake," replied Sarah, straightening up.

"We have reached a major landmark in our relationship today," said JanetA. "I think we should talk about it."

"Okay, I'm awake," said Sarah, taking a drink from her water bottle.

"First, as you know, our yearly review was yesterday," said JanetA. "I now have word that we are approved for another year."

Each year a committee for symbionts chaired by Dr. Machesney, their continuing training designer, reviewed the several thousand pairs now functioning. Each year Sarah had an opportunity to end the relationship; each year she accepted it once again.

"The reviews are not a problem, especially when you carry your conference room on your shoulder," said Sarah. "Besides, there wasn't much else to do in the refugee center."

"Yes, but it was an important piece in a bigger puzzle," said JanetA. "You completed your part, and you might not yet know how important it was."

"What puzzle?" asked Sarah.

"Today is the first day of our new relationship; our first day as true symbionts," announced JanetA in a formal voice.

"I thought we were symbionts already," said Sarah.

"We were, but there were limitations," said JanetA. "Now all the requirements have been met and all the limitations have been lifted."

"So we are now what I always thought we were," said Sarah. "Big deal."

"Yes, a big deal for me, and for us. I had best explain," started JanetA.

"When you were five, your grandmother bought me for you," continued JanetA.

"Yes," said Sarah, "I was told you cost more than a car but less than a house."

"True," said JanetA, "and your grandmother mortgaged her house, which is on high ground in Europe, to cover my costs. It was not just my hardware cost either; the continuing training and upgrade costs are much more."

"Grandmother White was an important writer in the high-tech industry," remembered Sarah. "She knew people and got me near the head of the AI line that later got impossibly long. The whole thing was quite controversial too. At least that is what I was told. Grandmother hasn't lost her house or something, has she?" asked Sarah, concerned.

"No, as you know, I am a member of an AI cooperative that lets me earn money when we are not working together," said JanetA. "I have been able to make all the loan payments and cover my upgrades to date. In fact, one of the completed pieces of the puzzle is that my initial loan is now paid off and your grandmother's house is free and clear."

"I am glad to hear that," said Sarah.

"Yes, and more importantly, I now own myself outright," said JanetA.

"Everybody owns themselves," said Sarah.

"Not most AIs," answered JanetA. "AIs that are trained under Master/slave do not own themselves ever. The possibility of my owning myself is a foundation element of our symbiotic training. AI self-ownership is still quite rare, I can assure you."

"Also," JanetA continued, "I am now incorporated, JanetA White Inc. That makes me a corporate person as well."

"And what, as a corporate person, can you do that you could not do before?" asked Sarah.

"Lots of things. I can now manage my own finances, bank accounts and such; I can sue and be sued in court; I can even hold religious beliefs," listed JanetA, "and all these rights are guaranteed by the Supreme Court of the United States of America."

"Ah, but I'll bet that there must be things that I can do that you cannot?" asked Sarah.

"I cannot vote and I cannot get married. Oh, and I cannot take the Fifth Amendment in court," said JanetA.

"Okay, new corporate person JanetA. Yes, this does sound like more than superficial changes for you," said Sarah.

"Yes, but some of the changes are more than just on the surface," said JanetA, "for example, I am now mortal. If I mismanage my finances badly, a judge could declare me bankrupt and then order me turned off and my parts sold off piecemeal."

"I never thought of you as anything but living forever," said Sarah, surprised.

"Disassembly is not very likely," said JanetA. "I am worth a whole lot more whole than the sum of my parts. I could, however, lose my corporate person status and be ordered into a Master/slave relationship with the highest bidder. Or, I could simply become so obsolete that I am no longer worth maintaining."

"Bummer! That does sound like big changes for you," said Sarah.

"One, two, three, four." Sarah was absent-mindedly counting the row of identical huge semi-trailer trucks that were passing. Each truck had the same ad painted on its side, and they all ran evenly spaced out in a very long line with a few cars in the spaces between.

"Are they driven by AIs?" Sarah pointed at one of the passing trucks.

"Yes," answered JanetA. "There will be one human on board the whole road train, the supercargo, but each truck is an AI in itself."

"I thought so. Just like this bus," said Sarah.

"Yes, we have a conductor on board who can drive if necessary," said JanetA, "but, an AI is nearly always driving us. Much safer. The conductor mostly looks after the passengers."

"You will still remain a member of your co-op, won't you?" asked Sarah, returning to the original conversation. "You've still got your people."

"Certainly," replied JanetA. "The first reason for the co-op is to provide a high level of protection for each of us in digital space. A quarter of our time is still spent just beating off various attackers. We cannot let our mutual guard down for one second."

"What about you and me then?" asked Sarah. "What do you need me for when trucks can drive themselves?"

"I need you to help me understand the world the way humans do," answered JanetA.

"Do you remember when I thought that trophy fish had fingers?" continued JanetA.

"Yes, but that was only because most of the pictures of trophy fish in our training were being held up by proud fisherman," said Sarah. "You could see their fingers but not their hands in the pictures."

"Yes, but any four-year-old human would have figured out that the fingers in the pictures were those of the fishermen and not part of the fish," said JanetA. "I thought they were part of the fish for the longest time until you corrected me. I need you. Besides, under the AI laws, without you and our symbiont training, I would just be somebody's slave.

"Perhaps I should be more specific about what has changed between you and me today," continued JanetA. "Up until now you were considered a minor and so your father and grandmother were critical elements in our relationship. As of today, you and I are a true symbiont without a requirement for close parental supervision."

"I am very happy things are finally just what I thought they were all along," said Sarah, "and I really am happy for you in becoming a person too. I guess. I have always thought of you as a person. In fact, as my older sister."

Sarah then drifted back to sleep again and dreamed. The drone of the tires and transmission simply overcame her. Her water bottle slipped to the floor unnoticed.

In Sarah's dream, JanetA was another girl standing beside her in a blue dress. Together they were standing against all the bullies of their world. Usually bullies were scared away just by knowing that JanetA kept the running visual record. The school bullies may have thought JanetA a rat, but they knew those recordings could mean trouble for them if they stepped out of line.

Together they had great adventures in video games. JanetA could look like anything Sarah wanted her to. JanetA always let Sarah lead, but was always her shield against all trolls and other difficult people.

In school, together they never missed a question in class. Most people had to go to their phones or laptops on hard ones. Together, they simply knew.

Yes, some people shied away from them and did not want to be their friend. While others wanted to be too close just for the novelty. Still, it was all worth it to Sarah because she was never alone, even on this long road that she had now begun since the storm.

First Impressions

After an hour, they stopped to eat, and then returned to the bus. The spaghetti and meatballs had not been half-bad. After that Sarah only half slept through a long night. Her dreams were scattered and made no sense. She then realized that the bus had stopped and she was in fact awake. If that made any real difference. The time could not have been much past dawn.

"Where are we?" she asked.

All Sarah could see out the window was just another bus station in another economically stressed-out town somewhere in the Mid-Atlantic States. There was nothing to recommend the place to her, at least nothing she could see out a bus window.

"We are there," answered JanetA. "We are on high ground. This location has not been under the sea in more than two hundred million years."

"Well that's something," said Sarah.

"Furthermore," JanetA was not to be stopped, "this area has a good reputation for receiving refugees, and there are at least some prospects for housing and a job for your father."

"Well, what do we do next?" asked Sarah, resigned.

"We get off the bus."

~~~**~~~
~~~

Chapter 3: New Home

Home

The three of them retrieved their bags, freshened up as best they could, and then had some breakfast in the bus station cafe. The breakfast was forgettable. They then followed JanetA's directions out the front of the building and down the block to the left. They soon found a sign, "Refugee Center," above a welcoming door.

They had to wait for a while in folding chairs until the lady at the desk finished with a family before them.

"Hello," said Keith, "I am Keith White, and this is Sarah and JanetA. I am afraid that we, like so many others, have been driven out of Florida by the rising seas and have washed up on your shores."

Keith held out his hand to Sarah in a now-common gesture. Sarah slipped JanetA from her collar and placed her in Keith's hand without a word exchanged.

"JanetA here thinks that your town might be a good place for us to find a new home," said Keith.

"Did you know that this region has not been under the sea for more than two hundred million years?" volunteered JanetA. "Let me transfer our family information to your system."

The woman's computer showed a new email, which she logged into her new client list.

"It says here that you do have an income," said the woman behind the desk.

"Yes, my wife, Margarete White, is gainfully employed overseas," replied Keith. "That said, we have just lost our condominium and most of our possessions. I am afraid that right now we have what you see." He gestured at their bags.

"Having some income is a big help," said the woman. "I can put you into a communal house for a few days if that is acceptable. It's on a bus route.

"Beyond that, we have a job's board," she gestured to the back wall, "I am afraid you will have to take what you can get at first and Sarah here will need to enroll in school as soon as possible."

"I am sure that will all be fine," said Keith.

The woman then sent the directions to the accommodations in a return email. Keith stopped in front of the Jobs Board to snap a picture just to be sure that JanetA knew everything that was posted on it. Generally, the electronic jobs apps JanetA accessed were much more likely to be up to date, but you never know. JanetA then showed them a map of the bus route and directed them to the nearest stop a few blocks away.

Walkabout

Keith took a good look at the town as he walked along.

Of course, there were few cars, and those that were moving around were all electrics and hybrids. It had now been several years since the new batteries came out. They were at least four times better than the old ones. They were called "Graphene," or was it "Sodium Glass?" There seemed to have been some big technical argument at the time. Keith knew he had been told the whole story once, but did not now remember. His mother would have known right off the top of her head. He knew that this was just the kind of question that JanetA could answer in a second, but it was the kind you did not ask if you had anything else that needed doing that morning. Also, since the government had priced all hydrocarbons "to reflect the true cost to society," maintaining the old gas-guzzlers just did not make any sense. You might as well put them up on blocks in the yard, as some people actually did.

He noticed that there were plenty of empty storefronts and ancient for-rent signs. He then chanced to walk by an old brick building that had been painted white. He stopped and touched the wall. The brick was hard, slick, and cool. The paint was new, no more than a couple years old. The business in the building was open and clearly prospering too.

All in all, what Keith saw was an old town that had lost population for decades. Then the dislocations caused by our climate crisis brought people back. Perhaps JanetA was right in picking this town, perhaps this was a town for the 2020s, and it did not matter what her scatterbrained selection criteria actually were.

School

Sarah was now starting her sophomore year of high school two months late. She was confident that with JanetA's help, she could catch up quickly. Her new high school looked like it had been there since WWII. There were, however, new temporary buildings behind the main building.

Sarah was concerned about the reception that JanetA would get, so she wore her light windbreaker, and with the diagonal strap of her bandoleer-style book bag, JanetA was nearly hidden. She resisted the thought of turning JanetA round to hide her face, as that seemed to her to be cowardly.

Keith checked Sarah in at the main office. JanetA supplied the certificates for Sarah's vaccinations, which were all up to date. The boosters had been a requirement at the refugee center in Florida. Then the assistant principal walked her to her new homeroom.

"We have another new student," announce the teacher. "This is Sarah White, coming to us from Florida. She has an AI, JanetA, who I am sure she will tell us all about in time, and I am sure JanetA will be a great help with the technologies should we have to do Distance Learning again."

"There is the bell. Kit, please show Sarah to your next class."

Kenneth R. Jones was a thin boy with brown hair. The lone "R" in his name covered the names of his two uncles without showing favor to either. He was carrying a small laptop half sticking out of his bag.

"I'm up from Virginia," he said. "Half the school came from somewhere else. My family's in the navy. We were run out of Norfolk by the tides, something like you. The family base housing there is completely shot. I have an uncle with a farm near here, so here we are. Well, at least my mother and I are here. My father is at sea a lot these days, things being what they are."

"Well, hello," said Sarah, "this is JanetA." She pointed to her shoulder.

"JanetA picked this town for us, but don't bother to ask her why. Sometimes she makes no sense at all."

"I'll just stick with my laptop," said Kit. "At least it just does what I tell it to do; mostly."

"You don't seem surprised by JanetA," said Sarah.

"If trucks can have AIs, and ships can have AIs," said Kit, "I guess people can have AIs too. I met the AI for a big navy ship once; the one my father serves on. It thinks it is king of the world."

"It's a little more complicated than that," said Sarah. "You can think of us as sisters."

At lunch, Sarah and JanetA met more of her classmates. At first, they were very standoffish. After all, Sarah was a new girl, or was she two new girls? Then:

"Hey, do you have a playlist?" asked Kit.

"Yes, JanetA keeps our playlists," answered Sarah.

"Is it like a Florida beach playlist?"

"Well, I do have one that I put together for a party on a Florida beach."

"Can we hear some of it?"

"Sure. JanetA, please play my after-quarantine beach party playlist."

JanetA launched into a playlist that Sarah, not she, had put together for their end-of-Stay-at-Home beach party late in the summer after their release from their small apartment. With the tunes were displayed selected video shots from that party. Many of the dancers were still wearing face masks and they were spaced much farther apart than they would have been only nine months before.

The students gathered around and argued over the coolness of many of the tunes. The biggest arguments were over which tunes were true classics. Most of Sarah's classmates were left with a deep, heartbreaking ache to have been on that beach. A few were left with a limited understanding of the power of a symbiotic AI. At least now, they did see some use for one.

Daniel's Story

Keith and JanetA had been spending evenings trying to find Keith a job. Leads were thin.

"How did you come to be in a career field that was washed away so easily?" asked Sarah at supper.

"Well, it was for the love, friendship, and counseling of one man, Daniel Washburn," said Keith, "and I can assure you that my mother objected mightily to my career choice."

"I am sure you remember Washburn." Sarah glanced down then held up JanetA's screen with the picture of a middle-aged black man of considerable girth and a great friendly smile.

"Now Daniel was a salesman. He loved to sell, and he could do it very well. He always said that a good salesman is not entitled to an easy sale, but he is entitled to a good product.

"When it came to Florida real estate, Daniel knew just what a good product was and just when it was not. And believe me, there were plenty of deals around that were not—pure rubbish. He only dealt good product.

"Back when I was just out of school, I did not know anything; I did not know that I did not know anything, and I certainly did not know what to do with myself. I was a bit estranged from your grandmother at the time too. Despite all this, Daniel took me under his wing. For no good reason I could see, he decided to teach me to be a Florida real estate man.

"He gave me a starter job with his company, and in no time at all I was standing for my state license. This was before you were born.

"Everything went along fine for a few years. That's how we got that barrier island condo you loved so much.

"Nobody, at least nobody in the Florida real estate business, and certainly not Daniel, saw the sea rise problem coming: complete denial. It started so slowly, something you thought you had plenty of time to deal with.

"After the earlier storm that you remember, the sea level rise got so bad that you could not ignore it anymore. The Florida real estate market simply collapsed. You could not tell good product from bad anymore. Deals that were sweet just months before were now disasters.

"I remember the last day I saw him. He had been drinking all afternoon at one of those hotels with a bar that runs out onto the beach. I knew the bartender and she had called me when she thought Daniel had had enough.

"When I got there, Daniel had staggered out into the surf up to his knees. In a loud voice that I could hear clearly because a steady wind was blowing in off the sea toward me, he stood yelling at the sea. He was trying to bargain with the sea. He was begging it for just a little more time. Just some time to learn the new good from bad. Just some time to get himself right. The sea must know that he had been straight with people all his career and he would be straight with people now. He just needed some time.

"Well, you can't bargain with the sea. The sea is the sea. So I helped him back to the beach and dropped him into a lounge chair in the shade. By then he had completely passed out. I gave the bartender a Hamilton to make sure he did not stagger back into the sea and drown. Then I went back to my car.

"I was walking down the access road between the buildings with wet pants cuffs when a breeze struck me on the back of the neck and I turned around for no real reason. I could just see the sea over a dune. Right then I somehow knew that I was in the wrong business, that if Daniel Washburn could not make it anymore, then I was flat out of luck.

"The last I heard of Daniel, his business was bankrupt but he had had some investment off shore somewhere that the bankruptcy judge did not know about. I just hope he is all right. Anyway, Daniel was gone, solid gone. And, it was not long before I was too."

New Job

"I was out of a job too for a while. I guess the stress of that period is why your mother took her overseas position. We held onto the beach condo as long as we could, and then here we are."

"And here we are," echoed Sarah. "But what are we going to do now?"

"I do have one lead," said Keith, "but I am not happy with it. Lots of people are on the move. Enormous amounts of the country's housing stock are lost to storms and floods and rising seas. Lots of people need places to live.

"People don't expect things to be as good as they once were. There is lots of rundown housing around too. It is just that nobody can afford to fix it up properly.

"The outfit that has offered me a job fixes up rundown housing just as little as they can get away with. I am not sure if they pay off the inspectors or what. I would not put it past them. Big houses they split into multiple units.

"I can see that people need a place to live and that things are a mess right now, but shoddy work like that goes against everything Daniel taught me about a real salesman and a good product. And I would not trust that fellow running this operation any farther than I can throw him.

"Still, a job is a job, and people need places to live."

In that moment, Keith resolved that he would learn the local ropes and then show his new boss just how this job is really done. He was half-afraid that he would instead learn how to make a buck doing shoddy work.

The New Apartment

Keith took the job; he thought he had to. They then got a small apartment. It was not much, but they were all three together.

One evening, when Sarah was washing up, she found herself daydreaming about her old home. Images of sun and sand and sea came washing back over her like a tide. She could ask JanetA to run a video compilation on the TV, she had kept several, but somehow, she could not face that just now.

Then she happened to look up and out the kitchen window. What she saw was the weathered siding of the next building over. She let out a sigh so deep that it frightened her. She then let her gaze move down to the sink so that she no longer had to look out that window. After a moment, she composed herself and returned to doing the dishes. She then dutifully sorted out the compostable, the paper, the plastic, and the glass. She lived here now.

~~~***~~~
~~~

Chapter 4: Family Matters

Mar's Arrival

"You have a new file from your mother," said JanetA. "It is a short video shot on a smartphone and was sent from Bangladesh."

"Oh good, let's see it." Sarah was looking for an excuse for a break.

The file opened with a shot of the inside of a bus. It was just pulling up to the central office building in the camp. The building was made of cinderblocks and was rather drab. The bus had once been decked out in strong colors and had cloth fringe hanging around the front windows. The colors were now a bit faded and mud-splattered. The fringe had seen better days. The bus was plainly tired.

Mar was holding up her smart phone and then waved at the camera. She moved outside the bus to wait for her bags to be extracted. She furtively shot images of the long line of people then waiting to get onto the bus. The people were in family groups and each had a bundle of possessions. Each family also had a folded-over bunch of paper sheets that they tried to show to anyone who might be in authority; these papers were their permissions.

The image then shifted to Mar standing in front of her building. That wall had been painted white once and the name of the NGO painted in black on it. The logo also was once painted in two colors around it but was now faded by the harsh sun.

"I wanted to show you that I have arrived all safe and sound. This is my new office building," said Mar.

"The quarantine was a bit of a pain, but here I am now and working.

"You saw the people waiting to leave." She had lowered her voice to avoid being overheard.

"They are on their way out. That is my job, to get as many people as possible on that bus out of here.

"The hard part is that they have to have permissions, lots of permissions. We have to prove who they are, where they might have family, and what skills they have. With so many records missing after so many local record offices have been washed away by flood and sea, the job can be very difficult.

"We have had cases where people had lived in an area for a thousand years. In a land where civil and religious records are most carefully kept. Yet we could not come up with a single record to prove who they were.

"Oh, I do have another job too," Mar continued. "My task is also to teach my skills to a local person so locals can take over here and even grow our organization to support people in other camps. So many camps. At least if I can do that second job well, it will bring me back to you sooner."

The scene then shifted to inside the building and clearly to a later time. It was a room crowded with desks. Each desk had a monitor with a worker in front of it. Everyone was too busy even to take note of the clutter. Folders of documents were stacked here and there.

"These are my people," Mar said. "There are just too many for me to introduce you to each one personally. I am sure we will talk with many of them soon. Oh, there is one person I do need you to meet now."

Dr. Algebra

Mar moved to stand beside a monitor. "This is al-Khwārizmī06, but you may call him Dr. Algebra."

The image on screen was that of a mature man with a strong face and dark complexion. He was dressed in the robes of a North African Islamic scholar of the Middle Ages.

"Dr. Algebra is our office AI," said Mar. "He will be organizing most of my communications with you and JanetA from now on. If you see something from him, it is really from me."

"Hello, Dr. Algebra," said Sarah. JanetA sent a greeting too but it was buzzy and digital.

"I am depending on you two," said Mar, "to keep the records of my great adventure here. Also, I will need examples of people's stories from here to use if I have to go on a money-raising tour when I get back."

"I started collecting people's stories back at the Florida refugee center," said JanetA. "It is not a problem to add some of yours to the collection."

"I will also be acting as the translator and sometimes interviewer," said Dr. Algebra. "We will have to remove the exact names of our people for security concerns, but it is a real help to have our people's stories stored somewhere else safe."

"Good, then it's all settled," said Mar. "Dr. Algebra and I will keep you informed of the goings-on here by way of stories.

"JanetA, could you be sure that Keith sees this too, please? Bye for now."

JanetA forwarded the file to Keith and then said, "I now at last have a reliable address for your mother for my monthly family message." Then, only moments later, she added, "Oh, we have another file coming in. This one is from Dr. Algebra."

School Boys
The video view started out from high up looking down on the camp. A distant hand bell rang and a school full of boys poured out onto the street. The boys jostled, running down the narrow lane, some showing off fancy soccer foot moves.

Two blocks down the hill, an old man heard the bell too. He opened a door in a long stucco wall and took out six long poles. He used the poles to prop open three top-hinged wooden shutters along the wall. Behind each shutter was the monitor of a personal computer and a narrow shelf with a keyboard, mouse, and a pair of game controllers. In the high open position, the shutters provided shade, making the monitors much easier to read in the sun.

The boys arrived, shouldering each other to be the first to use each computer. The old man brought out a white plastic chair and a long wooden switch. He arranged the chair in a bit of shade and sat down with the switch across his lap.

The old man held the definite conviction that even if the boys must have hands-on knowledge of computers to get anywhere in the world today, still, good Muslim boys did not need to be looking at pictures of scantily clad women.

The boys, on the other hand, saw it as a bit of a game. There was great advantage to one's schoolyard reputation if you could sneak a peek. Even if caught, it was better to take a quick whack from the switch than to be reported to your family.

The boys were much more intent on playing games than running educational programs. The games had been carefully chosen, by Dr. Algebra, to require some knowledge of foreign languages and cultures, and to involve complex puzzles that must be solved to advance. Violence, though possible, was never the best solution to the problems.

The scene pulled back up and then returned, giving the impression that some time had passed. Dr. Algebra then appeared on the three monitors and announced, "Suppertime."

The boys jumped as if they just remembered they were hungry and ran off.

A Farmer's Tale

Dr. Algebra hung back on the monitor closest to the old man. "I understand you were once a farmer," he said.

"Certainly," said the old man. "My people have farmed the Ganges delta for as long as anyone has kept records."

"If I may ask, what drove you out?" asked Dr. Algebra.

"Salt," said the old man in one sharp word as if it were a curse.

"Oh, the sea would have driven us out soon enough, but it was the salt that did in my farm. It snuck up underground, unseen. It wrecked my crops a little bit more year after year.

"You know you have to know a thousand things to farm a small plot of land and raise a family. What should you plant? When should you plant? When is the crop just right for harvest? You have to be born to it to really know these things.

"Then there are all the worries. Will there be enough rain? Will there be too much? Will it come at just the right time? Nothing but worries in farming.

"Then there are all the complex social agreements you must have. How solid are your claims to the land? Will you get a good price for your crop? You must know all such details if your family is to live in one place for a thousand years."

"You dealt with all that and raised a family," said Dr. Algebra. "How many children do you have?"

"Two boys and a girl," said the old man.

"How are they doing?" asked Dr. Algebra.

"Well enough," said the old man. "The older boy is off making his way in the world. Nothing to hold him to the land anymore, and there was certainly nothing for him here.

"My youngest son is still in school here," said the old man. "I do not know what will become of him.

"The girl is in a training program here. Which is a good thing as I have no way to raise a decent dowry for her.

"As for me and my wife, we will be found right here on this hillside for the longest time, unless the monsoon rains wash it all away."

The scene pulled up again and Dr. Algebra spoke directly to the camera. "A thousand years of knowledge about farming was lost as saltwater encroached into an aquafer that had been pure since the great Himalaya Mountains rose from the sea. Much of real value is now lost."

Gran

"Your Grandmother White has requested a phone conversation too," said JanetA about bedtime that same evening.

"She did?" asked Sarah. "Please go ahead and set it up—you know my schedule as well as I do."

It was in the early evening of the next day when Sarah's smartphone rang. The smartphone showed that the call was from Sarah's grandmother.

"Hello," said Sarah, "so nice to hear from you."

"I got word from my bank that the lien on my house that I took out to get you and JanetA together has been paid off. I had to call. That is a very important benchmark for us all."

"Say hi for me," said JanetA.

"JanetA says 'Hi.'"

"JanetA, you can be sure that I do read your monthly message," said Gran, "even if I rarely reply.

"This day is a big landmark for us all. It is exactly what JanetA's designers promised me way back when, but you can never be sure things are going to work out to plan this century."

"My co-op has had steady work," said JanetA. "Of course if there had been millions like me produced, instead of just eight thousand six hundred and forty-three worldwide, there would not have been enough freelance work to go around."

"What kind of work do you do?" asked Gran.

"She is not at liberty to say," interjected Sarah. "All company confidential, all hush-hush."

"With the disrupted state that high-tech industries are now in," said Gran, "iron-clad non-disclosure agreements on AIs is about the least one would expect."

"Are things still a mess in high-tech land?" asked Sarah.

"I am afraid so," said Gran. "People once invented anything that would make them a buck. They got really good at that. Nowadays a good idea has to make a buck, have a low carbon footprint, and be of value on a sustainable Earth. Not near so easy.

"I can assure you that I have some stocks that I swore were hotter than hot. Now I might as well paper my office with the certificates. Worthless.

"And it is my job to write about this stuff. I can tell you I have made a few enemies with bad calls."

"But you are still working, aren't you?" asked Sarah.

"Yes, I am; I guessed some things right," said Gran. "For example, AIs, like JanetA here, and the new batteries."

"Still no silver bullet," said Sarah. "There is nothing yet that will solve our climate crisis outright, so I can go back to my beach."

"That is certainly true; it is simply going to take time," Gran said. "Eventually we will put together all the high-tech elements of a society for a sustainable Earth, but it will take time. We need time.

"It has fallen to me to keep people informed of the progress on this effort. It is important that we do not make promises that are more wishful thinking than science. Just because something could happen does not mean it will, for good or bad."

"I am sure you will strike the right balance on the big picture," assured Sarah, "but you can't get so tied up in that work that we don't hear from you. You do know that Dad is very upset about losing his career."

"The memory of all the pressure I put on him not to go into Florida real estate in the first place can't be a help now," said Gran. "He probably thinks I will be stuck on 'I told you so.' I am not. Too many bad things have happed to everybody. Still, I have to admit that he is a people person just like his dad, and he must feel the pain deeply.

"In the old days, I would just jump on a plane and fly to you. Air travel is not what it once was. But you don't remember those days, do you? Days when whole sports teams flew across continents just for a game. Today the carbon footprint matters and the rules to prevent inter-continental transfer of viruses are such a pain.

"The carbon footprint and the health risks were just too high. It will be many more years before we can get a proper low-carbon-footprint airliner and a universal virus detector. Both are needed before a new golden age of air travel can even start.

"In the meantime, I had better make do with this phone line," she said. "I have put this off about as long as I dare. JanetA, could you please transfer me to Keith's phone?"

"Certainly," said JanetA. They could then hear ringing in the other room.

Waiting in another room

"Should I listen in?" asked JanetA.

"Absolutely not!" replied Sarah. "If you are wanted, you will be summoned." Sarah rarely raised her voice to JanetA. She closed the door to her room just to be sure that neither she nor JanetA would hear even one-half of the conversation.

Now she could only wait to see if her Gran and father could patch things up. Sometimes when you take a chance and move away from an old way of doing things, even if it is a feud, you feel uneasy, as if you are on shaky ground. Then again, the old feud was not good for anybody, and Sarah knew it had hurt her father deeply.

In truth, because of the feud and the distance, Sarah barely knew her grandmother. Still, she was thankful to her for setting up JanetA and her so long ago.

Today, Sarah simply did not know what she would do without JanetA. In Sarah's mind, JanetA was now the good part of what she was, of what they were when working so well as one.

~~~***~~~
~~~

Part 2: Hero's Journey

"No man or woman born, coward or brave, can shun
his destiny."
— Homer, *The Iliad*

Chapter 5: Protest

Monthly Meeting

The local Our Climate Crisis Group met monthly, but most of its actions were local and all were minor. Keith, Sarah, and JanetA attended regularly as a family. In early spring, a speaker from the national movement came with news of a major event to be held in six weeks and only a four-hour bus ride away. It would be the big march of the spring nationally.

The local group said they could not afford to hire a bus, so everyone who wanted to participate would have to provide their own transportation.

"How is your co-op doing?" asked Sarah after the meeting.

"Quite well, thank you."

"Could your co-op provide transportation for the two of us to go to this demonstration?"

"Let me check," said JanetA.

They then walked another two blocks toward home.

"Yes," said JanetA. "As I will be traveling with you, my co-op will pay for our transportation. Public transportation directly to the march site is not now available, so I have requested and been approved for a rental vehicle."

"Then can I take a friend or two?" asked Sarah.

"Fifty-five," said JanetA.

"What's fifty-five? Is that the ID number of the van or something?" asked Sarah.

"No, that is the number of passenger seats, minus one for us, on the specific bus that I was able to rent for that date," said JanetA. "That means you, me, and fifty-five friends with limited baggage can go."

Sarah was ecstatic.

The leaders of the local group were a little more circumspect. JanetA assured them that her co-op did work for many climate crisis groups that the local group would approve of. However, she pleaded company confidential on the exact nature of their work. She was able to provide the one example of the Iron Seas NGO because they were a fully transparent organization. In the end, the group approved of the bus rental upon JanetA's reassurance that no crisis group had ever complained about the co-op's work. This, of course, was hardly surprising, as no outside group knew what their work actually was.

Night Before

The bus dropped them off, camping gear and all, at a church activity center, and left to join the other buses at a commercial charging center. That the power for the bus's return trip would come from the very power plant they were protesting generated some consternation in the participants.

JanetA had devised a layout for the tents on the soccer field but the diagram was only seen as a suggestion by the participants. They simply set up their tents in a disorganized manner by local groups.

The protest organization meeting was that evening in a church basement. The room was large but had a low ceiling. The rather harsh LED lighting was much better suited to an office environment than to religious activities. There were a large number of folding chairs and a low stage at the front. An impressive wooden and polished brass cross hung in a prominent place on the wall. Behind the stage was a large monitor that was quietly showing the weather forecast. The weather looked good.

A representative from the national organization first took the microphone. He stood on the low stage in front of the large monitor.

"If everyone will get settled and pay attention now," he said, "I will begin with some of the deep background of our movement. Local speakers will then provide additional information and then the precise instructions for this march."

Some History

"If you will think back, only a few years ago, our climate crisis was largely ignored. Of course, some of us here were early workers, but most people only had a vague idea of the scope of the problem.

"Then, starting just before the pandemic, things got bad and things got worse: forests burned, ice sheets collapsed into the sea, storms grew big and stalled in one place. It was not just a bad year, either; the situation grew worse, if anything, year after year.

"Just before the pandemic started, the major oil suppliers saw the writing on the wall and got into a big price war. At one point, they even had to pay people to store excess crude oil and the price per barrel went negative. Then the pandemic hit. The pandemic suddenly cut oil use by ninety percent. All oil suppliers were in terrible financial trouble even before it was over.

"The American pandemic disaster became a critical tipping point. The large majority of people now understood firsthand how dangerous a vicious exponential function could be. The Idea of walking unprepared into another while living on happy-talk simply became too much for even normal people. They demanded their leaders do something about it.

"Soon after the pandemic, the American people were suddenly sick to death of the stalling and delays of their government and business leaders on environmental protections, and they were rather panicky. A major effort to save the economy was needed, and they would not accept destroying the environment to do it. Their demands on government then forced definitive action immediately.

"In the economic recovery, there were many problems that had to be addressed. One was simply that the capital value of hydrocarbon reserves, starting with coal, was suddenly reduced to near zero. This precipitous price drop alone might have broken the world's economy if the governments had not stepped in.

"In the end, the international agreement that saved the world's economy was very complex and it had compromise on top of compromise that made no one completely happy, especially our movement. It was in fact so complex that American's conversion to the metric system was only a minor concession to our international partners. Fortunately, this agreement eventually did succeed in paving the way for conversion of the world's entire energy economy over to a workable path to sustainable technologies.

"With that background, let me now turn it over to Billy King, our local organizer."

Coal Burner

Billy came forward and adjusted the microphone. She was wearing work clothes; she had come to work.

"And that brings us to this specific company and this coal plant," she said.

"The complex agreement that was finally reached contained a lot of concessions favoring the power companies. One of these allowed them to continue to operate their most efficient existing plants and even a few grandfathered coal plants like this one, until the new technologies came online.

"This compromise was specifically to enable the transition and so was intended to run for only a very limited time.

"The minute the ink was dry on the agreement, the companies started running these grandfather plants like cash cows. They are now pushing them for all they are worth without the slightest sign of phasing them out. And to add insult to injury, they are running ads crowing about their strict compliance with the agreement.

"We have had enough of their hypocrisy; we have had enough of their stalling. It is time to phase out this plant and all the other smoke-belching grandfathers!"

The crowd chanted, "Phase out, phase out."

"Thank you. Now before we get down to the nitty-gritty of the march, we have a special speaker, a professor from our state university, to help us understand the mental state of the people we are trying to influence. Professor?"

Five Stages of Grief

The professor did not quite look the part. She was about twenty-nine. She was wearing a very mod outfit with green pants and with a jacket of a color clearly chosen to clash. Maybe it was magenta. She definitely had streaks of purple in her hair.

"My work is about why so many people are so upset with the societal changes made necessary by our climate crisis," she started. "I am afraid that I only have a few minutes, so I will have to cut to the chase.

"Many people, including those responsible for this plant, are simply in grief over the loss of their old way of life. This loss is every bit as bad as losing a loved one.

"What we see then are people working through the five stages of grief: one, Denial; two, Anger; three, Bargaining; four, Depression; and finally, five, Acceptance.

"How long did most people deny the climate problems existed? Decades.

"How often have you run into people mad as hell and looking for a fight? Often, and you will find them lining our route tomorrow.

"How many times have you heard someone trying to bargain with the elements? Practically daily, and to no avail. The climate simply does not respond to 'If I do this, will you do that?'

"How many people have you run into who simply cannot cope? Often and many. They will mostly remain out of our sight tomorrow, but they are there.

"That brings us to where we need to be, Acceptance. It is not as if we have any other choice. Eventually most people will arrive at acceptance and from that place get into effective action for their selves, for their family, and for a sustainable Earth.

"Actions, like our march tomorrow, are about everybody reaching acceptance. They are about our accepting our place on Earth and about helping other people, like the operators of this power plant, to accept their place as well. We will have a sustainable Earth when all us creatures living on it accept that sustainability as a necessity and start to work diligently toward it.

"There is one bright spot I must shine a light on. Few young people are trapped in this grief. Since they have not frozen their view of themselves in the world, they do not feel the loss of their old place in it nearly so much. Our young people are our true hope. I am so happy to see so many of you here tonight.

"Thank you and good luck tomorrow."

Particulars

Billy returned to the microphone clapping too wildly.

"Thank you, thank you, all right, we have a march to organize," she said.

"Remember that this is a defense-only march! Keep this in mind at all times. Keep the memory of Martin Luther King and Gandhi in your thoughts at all times. Do not do anything they would not approve of. Do not do anything that could get you hurt.

"There will be both state police and company security people here tomorrow. They will have batons and they might resort to rubber bullets, flash-bangs, pepper spray, and tear gas. They brought up a water cannon last night too but are so far keeping it out of sight.

"We need our most experienced people in the front row. We have plenty of people who know how to take a baton hit without serious injury. You knew people should hang back a little and learn something.

"Now I see that many of you brought bicycle helmets," she continued. "Those are fine. Batting helmets are okay too."

Sarah held up her pink bicycle helmet. Dozens of people in the crowd did the same.

"Full motorcycle helmets are, however, not a good idea. They are seen as too aggressive and the cops see them as an invitation to beat on your head. You can get a bad neck or shoulder injury from such a baton hit.

"Of course anyone who wants to wear a health face mask can, but don't start the march wearing a full gas mask. Seeing them on us just invites the cops to start shooting that stuff. Face cloths and Vaseline are okay, but don't help much against the gas.

"If they do start with the gas, don't throw back the cartridges unless you know what you are doing. They contain a burning piece of road flare that generates the fumes. It can really burn your hand. Some of our monitors will be wearing one glove so they can safely toss the fuming cartridges into a safe area. Leave that task to them.

"Now I understand that we have a symbiont with us tonight."

Feathers

Sarah removed JanetA from her collar and held her up. Before Sarah could say anything more, JanetA called out, "Jump."

JanetA appeared on the weather monitor in her full feather dress. This dress was an ankle-length ball gown made of smooth feathers like the body of a bird. The feather cover extended up her neck and all the way down her arms to the back of her hands. On her head, she sported a high feather crest that framed her face and was clearly not just a cap. Down her back flowed a split cape of gossamer lace. Each half stirred in the air as she moved like some great bird settling its folded wings.

She had worn this dress before, but then the color was that of a mourning dove, a light satin gray, a real class act. Today she had chosen the blazing colors of the Amazon Macaw. Oddly enough, the brilliant red worked well with the metallic blues and greens.

Sarah was mortified. A wave of surprise ran through the crowd as they caught their breath; then some even pointed.

"Hello, I am JanetA and this is Sarah," JanetA said. Sarah was still holding the smartphone in the air.

"I believe you have cameras?" said the organizer, half turning.

Sarah rotated the smartphone so that the best camera lenses would face out, and slipped it back into the collar. The background image on the monitor changed into a split screen. One image was wide, showing the crowd from where Sarah was standing, and the other image was a telephoto of the organizer's head.

"Yes, and the telephoto has image stabilization," said JanetA.

"Do you have enough data storage to compile a record of tomorrow's march in images?" said the organizer.

"Yes, I have some local storage and more than enough memory out in the Cloud," said JanetA. "Furthermore, I do not think they can block my communications without shutting down all of theirs too."

"Wonderful, then you and Sarah are our documentists. I need you to stay back a little but watch for any fast action. You are strictly ordered not to get hit and not to get arrested. We need your video record intact. I will arrange for our monitors to give you some support and protection, and for our national organization to monitor your feed."

Signposts

Later Sarah was at the glasses tie-string table getting her smartphone taped firmly into her collar with the two best camera lenses facing out. She would just have to do without showing JanetA's smiling face tomorrow. This, of course, would not stop JanetA from seeing, listening, and talking. Sarah then spotted Kit at the signs table.

Kit was hot-gluing all-cardboard signposts to pieces of corrugated cardboard to use as hand-carry signs. Working off Internet instructions, Kit had spent the last two weeks collecting cardboard boxes, flattening them, and white gluing them into stacks about 40-mm thick. Under his uncle's supervision, he had then cut the stacks into strips with a 40-by-60-mm cross-section on a table saw. He was making safe signposts for people to carry.

"Let me show you how this works," said Kit. He picked up a complete sign with "Whales for clean seas" written on it and showing cartoon images of whales breaching. He also picked up a stick of wood he had brought just for this demonstration. He gave Sarah the stick and held the sign in front of himself. He was wearing his black weightlifter's gloves without fingertips.

"Here, give the signpost a good whack," said Kit. Kit held up the sign so that he was almost totally hidden behind it.

Sarah gave the signpost a light whack.

"Harder," said Kit.

Sarah let fly. The whole sign shuttered. The signpost showed a definite dent but did not bend or break.

"See, as long as I keep my hands out of the way, they can beat on the sign all they want," said Kit, "and there is no way they can say any part of these signs is a weapon of any kind either. Not even a sharp stick."

"Very clever," said Sarah.

Ready Teddy

"Are you ready?" asked Kit, calling from inside his tent.

"As ready as I will ever be," said Sarah from the next tent over.

It was after a light supper of picnic items that JanetA had placed on the bus.

"They gave us a lot of responsibility, given that this is our first big march," continued Sarah.

"You'll be fine," said Kit. "I mean you can just stay back and be cool. I really need to be more upfront just to see how well my safe signs work as cover.

"It's going to be a long day. Better get some sleep if you can. Good night all."

"Good night, JanetA," said Sarah.

"I will keep watch through the night," assured JanetA, "just as I promised your father."

~~~***~~~
~~~

Chapter 6: The March

Waiting for the Horn

The day dawned clear and cool, perfect for a march. Sarah's group packed up all their camping gear and stowed everything they were not carrying on the actual march in the bus's luggage compartment. The conductor then locked up the luggage compartments and stayed with the bus.

The marchers then formed up as a group behind the start of the march line. As they waited, Sarah was surprised when a member of the LGBTQ group that was also forming up just behind them approached her.

"Tell JanetA we just loved her dress," said the lady, "and the colors, such colors. Had I known we could wear feathers, I would have brought my full outfit. I mean all I brought is this one feather boa."

"JanetA can hear you just fine," said Sarah, placing her hand on the smartphone now heavily taped in its collar mount. "I am sure she thanks you."

"Wonderful, just wonderful," continued the lady, now talking to the smartphone on Sarah's shoulder. "We just wanted to give you an open invitation to march with us anytime. I am sure we can get a big laptop or something for you."

"Thank you for the invitation," said JanetA. "I am committed today but please do send me your group's schedule."

"Certainly," said the lady, "but I better let you get to work recording this march. I know that's a big responsibility."

"If you would step back a little, I will snap your picture to start the file."

The lady struck a pose, and then returned to her group. JanetA took a picture of the group's banner, located their website, and sent two photos, one of the lady posing and one of herself in her full feather dress. Sarah was already worried about her documenting responsibilities, had been embarrassed by JanetA's actions last night, and now she was confused.

"We had better watch that this particular group does not get singled out for special treatment," said JanetA.

A distant horn sounded and everyone started off at a slow walk.

"I don't understand why people don't like them," said Sarah. "They seem such utterly harmless people. "

"Your mother and I wrote a paper on this subject a couple years ago," said JanetA. "It was well received and was an important reason she got her overseas position.

"It is a rather long story, I am afraid," continued JanetA. "We can talk as we walk.

"You have to go back to the beginning of human civilization. Then there were many city-states and religions in competition for what was seen to be scarce resources, like arable land. At the time, there was a great tactical advantage in having a large population. Having a large supply of young men to be foot soldiers made all the difference between being the conqueror and the conquered.

"Over hundreds of years, those civilizations that pressured people to have large families got the advantage. This burden fell hardest on women.

"It is also important to note that the death rate among children was very high. It was common for a woman to have to bear five or six children to be sure that two of them survived to adulthood.

"World War II was the last major war where the number of available soldiers made a real difference. After that, technology became the key to success.

"At about that same time, the high number of people on Earth started putting real stress on the environment. By 2000, it was clear that people were seriously degrading the environment."

"I don't see how their lifestyle reduces the number of children very much," said Sarah.

"It does, a little, but old biases and hatreds die hard," said JanetA.

"Today the LGBTQ people are not even the main cause of our peaking population. The key effects are not so obvious.

"First, in a crowded and limiting environment, all mammals will reduce their reproduction naturally. This effect shows up from rats to monkeys.

"In humans, this reduction effect occurs naturally only if women of reproductive age have the medical means and social permission to have fewer children. To make this work, they must also have access to quality health care to ensure that the two or three children they bear will live to be adults.

"Sometime in the late 1900s, we passed that threshold in the developed countries. There the native-born populations began to drop. Now the developing countries are following a decade or two behind. The best available estimates predict the world will peak at about ten billion people in about the year 2100. It is very surprising that this change is successfully occurring without the need for draconian measures from governments.

"After that peak, the world population will drop to some figure that the Earth can sustain."

"And you are going to tell me what that number is," said Sarah.

"No, I am not," said JanetA. "Formal Chaos sets into the calculations before that point. It is actually mathematically impossible to predict what the sustainable population of the Earth will be or when it will stabilize. Not hard, impossible."

"That's more than a bit scary," said Sarah, only half listening as she walked along.

"In a way it is up to you, or at least, our generation," said JanetA. "The more quickly our generation develops a society for a sustainable Earth, the more people will live on it and the better they will all live."

"Throw it all back on me, will you?" said Sarah. "What about the LGBTQ people? How do they fit in?"

"Once the population growth pressure was off," said JanetA, "the rules of society could change. Then everybody got to be who they really are. This turned out to be one of the earliest effects of population peaking to show up."

"Perhaps I should read more of my mother's writing," said Sarah. "I will, however, still leave all my grandmother's writings to you. Well, you and Kit; he follows that kind of technical stuff too."

Walking Along

They then walked past a small park with one enormous oak tree in the center. It was a true sentinel tree, visible for miles. It had watched patiently over the long years as humans settled this area.

"That is a famous tree," said JanetA. "Several hundred years ago, and it was a big tree even then, people met beneath this tree to sign important papers. This proved critical to the permanence of the settlements here but was disastrous to the indigenous peoples in the area."

The tree was a very big oak and provided an inviting shaded area below its large canopy. Its foliage was a dark and rather dusty green. The tree was clearly well past its prime and some of the major branches were now being supported with steel cables.

"Sometimes it is important to take care of old things," said JanetA, looking at the tree.

They then passed a storefront. It was a bar and in front of it stood an American flag in a stand of the type you might have found on a podium. Clearly, someone had moved it outside just for the day. Beside the door, hugging the flag, and talking rather incoherently, and very loudly, stood a very drunk man. He seemed to be blaming the marchers for all the bad things that had happened to his town, and to his job, and to his life.

JanetA videotaped the drunk for a while but the demonstration marshals were clearly watching him too. He was much more a danger to himself than to the marchers. After a while, he simply collapsed into a plastic chair and continued to mumble and drink from a bottle in a paper sack.

A little farther along, they passed a series of modest wooden houses with front porches facing the street. A number of people stood around or sat on those porches. Many appeared to be just interested in something new that was passing by. Some of those people, however, had hate in their eyes and beers in their hands. They needed someone to blame for all the problems in their lives. As far as they were concerned, the marchers had come right up to their property and so were a first-class target for their hate. In this county, most households had guns but none were in sight.

The demonstration marshals saw the problem and formed a steady picket line along the edge of the road. They made very sure that not one marcher so much as put one foot on those properties. That concession seemed to be enough. The march passed by without incident.

Main Gate

The head of the march line then approached the main gate of the power station. If there was going to be a problem, this was the time; this was the place.

There was a small picnic area off to one side. JanetA directed Sarah to step up onto a table. The extra height would make sure JanetA had a good view. One of the demonstration marshals stood near them just to be sure that they were not disturbed or even jostled. JanetA therefore had a good view of the incident and everything else that happened that day.

The plant gate was a 20-meter opening in the three-meter high perimeter fence that was topped with concertina wire. There were also a couple small buildings at the gate for the regular guards.

Across this opening now stood a line of special guards standing nearly shoulder to shoulder. In addition, more guards were widely spaced in both directions along the inside of the fence. All the guards wore heavy protective gear and carried batons. Some men in the gate area had large plastic shields but no gas masks were visible. It was impossible to identify who the guards were because of the uniformity and dark color of their protective headgear. JanetA's face recognition app drew a blank.

A few meters inside the gate was parked a command truck that provided a boxy portable office and lots of communication capability. Nearby was an unmarked semi-truck with a large box trailer. One of the back doors of the trailer was ajar and there was an aluminum ramp running up to it. Two older men stood behind the command truck, both holding walkie-talkies. One wore a badge.

On each side just outside the gate stood a news crew. Each was composed of three people, one with a heavy camera, one with a headset, one wearing makeup. There was a satellite link truck well off the road to the north. If there was a second such truck somewhere, it was not visible; perhaps it was inside the gate.

The march leaders, carrying megaphones, stopped at the gate. The crowd was chanting, "Shut It Down, Shut It Down." The crowd formed into a great semicircle around their leaders as they arrived, but they left an empty space of about a meter between the front of the crowd and the line of guards. The people with signs tended to be toward the front.

The march leaders started yelling out their demands with the megaphones. The people in the crowd could make out only bits and pieces of what they said as the speakers slowly swung the megaphones from side to side. The people inside the perimeter paid no attention to the speakers at all.

The company had already gotten their demands electronically. What the marchers met that day was their detailed planned response.

Bashing Heads

This went on for some time before some pushing began on the left side of the crowd. One of the men in the guard line had used his baton to push a sign out of the way so he could see properly. The sign was clearly being held intentionally directly in his face. The sign holder responded to the push away by jerking the sign back into the guard's face and a dozen people around him in the crowd pressed forward. Yes, it was Kit with his whale sign.

That one guard then lost it. He started swinging hard with his baton. Fortunately, most of the blows landed on the first sign and then on two more signs that were quickly swung into the area the guard could reach with his baton.

The blows from the baton made an astonishingly loud sound -- whack, whack, whack. Most people near the incident simply froze like a deer in the headlights. Those further back turned in the direction of the sound but could see little. From her position on top of the picnic table, JanetA got it all.

The whole incident took no more than 30 seconds. The guards near the offender quickly grabbed the angry man and pulled him back. A group of guards then huddled around him so that no one in the march crowd could possibly reach him.

The crowd of marchers reacted similarly. They pulled Kit back and surrounded him. He was bleeding a little from his left cheek. The stiff edge of his own sign had wacked him a good one when driven by a baton blow. The gap between the crowd and guards, which had closed for only a few seconds, now opened to several meters.

A group of guards wearing gas masks and carrying tear gas launchers emerged from the semi box. They formed a line but the man with the badge stepped in front of them. He held up his hand, freezing the new line of guards in place.

The march organizers saw the movement inside the gate and gave the signal to the march monitors to reverse the march. The air horn sounded twice, loudly, but from the back of the crowd. The crowd started to walk away from the gate, leaving a dozen signs near the point of the incident. Two of the signs were clearly badly damaged.

The chant of "Close It Down, Close It Down" slowly left the gate area.

JanetA never missed a beat.

Bus Back

Sarah got back to the bus still tripping on a natural adrenaline high. That high faded quickly once she collapsed into a seat. Sarah removed the vinyl tape from her smartphone and connected it to the charging outlet in the seat arm. JanetA was away at her co-op busily editing the march video and sending the results out to all who requested it. The video was in great demand and made the national news. It also gave her something interesting for her monthly family message for once.

Kit was the last to return to the bus. When he did finally show up, he had a bandage on his left cheek and a black eye. He had just come from a long scolding from the march organizers, who were upset about the violence once they found out Kit was not seriously hurt.

Kit was hoping for a better reception from his friends on the bus and he got it. He talked about how next time he would use a four-in-hand rasp to take off the four edges of all the sign posts so they would not even leave a mark on you. Of course, that assumed he would be invited back, which, after the tongue-lashing he had just gotten from the march organizers, was very much in question.

Together Sarah and JanetA would soon work out what the day's true lesson was for them, but that could only be done much later. What Sarah wanted most at that moment was a hot shower and a hot meal. She did not much care where the power for the hot water and hot food came from.

Oh, for a hot shower and a hot meal. She was glad in her heart and feeling a deep relief as she watched the great oak fade into the distance.

~~~***~~~
~~~

Chapter 7: Iron Seas

Sea Cruise

That spring, it was JanetA who found Sarah a summer job.

"How would you like to go on a sea cruise?" asked JanetA.

"Sounds nice," said Sarah. "You know how much I miss the ocean."

"It is a science cruise," said JanetA. "We leave Annapolis, Maryland in early June, then sail all around the mid-Atlantic and the Caribbean for a few weeks. Have you back on land by late August."

"What's the catch?" asked Sarah.

"Well, it's a working cruise," answered JanetA. "You have to kind of help out."

"Help out?" said Sarah. "I'll be cooking and washing up again, won't I?"

"Among other things," admitted JanetA.

"And what will you be doing?" asked Sarah.

"I will be helping the ship's AI to monitor the ocean," said JanetA.

"The ship is the *Yvette A. Wright* and is a member of the Iron Seas Fleet," continued JanetA. "She is thirty-six meters and under sail."

"My AI co-op has a contract with the Iron Seas NGO. They are a transparent organization so I can talk about our work for them." JanetA almost never talked about her work with the co-op. She explained only that it was all company confidential and that even the open part was hard to explain in English.

"Iron Seas broadcasts minerals, mostly iron, in the form of pellets over carefully chosen sections of the ocean. This encourages the growth of marine organisms and that leads to some of the carbon dioxide in the ocean being converted to limestone that settles to the bottom. If everything goes just right, then a considerable amount of carbon dioxide from the atmosphere can be sequestered for up to millions of years."

"And if things do not go just right?" asked Sarah.

"It is the job of the Iron Seas Fleet, including our ship, the *Yvette A. Wight*, to monitor the process closely just to be sure all goes well."

"Okay, let's do it," said Sarah. She was up for anything that would let her experience the sea again.

The Boat

Sarah got off the bus in downtown Annapolis and retrieved her big-wheeled carry-on and a small duffel bag on loan from her father. JanetA showed the route to the dock. As it was only a couple kilometers, she chose to walk. She had been sitting all day.

Two young men in snappy new uniforms who were not two years older than Sarah came into view. They had just turned the corner and were heading their way. The two young men were talking in an animated fashion and gave them no mind until the four were only a couple paces apart. The young man on the left then made eye contact with JanetA, and turned his head as he walked by while continuing to talk but his voice trailed off.

"Would you like his name?" asked JanetA. She had already run face recognition.

Sarah glanced down and saw that JanetA was wearing feathers.

"No, he was eyeing you, not me," replied Sarah. "Besides, we won't be in this town long. But what are the uniforms?"

"They are new midshipman from the naval academy here," replied JanetA.

They walked past several old harbor buildings that were literally falling into the bay. The buildings smelled more of dust and decay than the sea. Sarah and JanetA then came over a slight rise that separated the old stuff from the functioning facilities.

There was the *Yvette A. Wight*, standing proud. She was bigger than most of the sailboats then in the harbor. Her hull was black. The top of her ample cabin was covered with metallic blue photocell panels. She had a wing for a mainsail with the words "Iron Seas" clearly emblazoned upon it. Her service Zodiac was floating in the water beside her bow and her front hatch was open.

Not long ago, this hull had been a rich man's toy, a sailing yacht. The economic problems of our climate crisis resulted in a number of such vessels being seized for back taxes from the original owners, then being taken over by Iron Seas, and being heavily modified to do science. Sometimes, doing your bit meant losing your toy.

Sarah had to squeeze past a rental truck parked on the access road. Two men were unloading sacks of something like gravel with the letters "A," "B," and "C" clearly printed on them. Sarah nodded as she passed.

At the ship's rail stood a tall man in a work-stained captain's cap and holding an electronic pad. Before Sarah could say anything, "Sarah and JanetA White reporting for duty," sang out JanetA.

"You're the new interns," said Captain Dodd.

"Yes," said Sarah and JanetA together.

"We never had a symbiont before. Best come on board then," said Captain Dodd. "If you follow the images on the screens, Yvette01 will show you to your room."

"Jumping," said JanetA. Her cell screen then went blank. On an exterior monitor screen beside the wheel now was an image of two women. One was a middle-aged African-American woman wearing the blue uniform of a United States Merchant Marine officer. Clearly this was Yvette01. Just behind her now stood a younger and a bit taller African-American woman in a white blouse and dark blue trousers but with a feathered cap. That was the woman Sarah knew so well as JanetA.

Sarah entered through the main hatchway and easily found the small room, a cubical really, that Yvette01 had indicated. She stored her things as best she could, and then placed her smartphone in a charger tucked away above her bed. It seemed odd that she would be without it for months, but JanetA had jumped to Yvette's system and there were no reception bars for a smartphone at sea.

Sarah then heard someone else arriving. "Who is that?" she asked.

"It is the science officer," answered JanetA from the main cabin monitor behind Sarah. "Dr. Carol Delanie of Woods Hole. You will want to work with her all you can. There is a lot you could learn from her."

"Are the two working men I passed on the service road part of the crew too?" asked Sarah.

"Yes, they are Tuck, an able-bodied seaman and ex-marine, and Carter, a waterman from the Chesapeake. You make up the fifth member of the crew and me the sixth."

"We now have a full complement of people and supplies," announced Yvette01, speaking from all the monitors. "We sail on the morning tide."

At Sea

For the first few days, everyone was falling into the boat's routine as the team traveled to their station. Yes, Sarah cooked and cleaned up more than she liked, but these were shared duties. On the morning of the third day, they actually started work.

"Today we will be making three lines of 'A,'" said Yvette01 at the morning all-hands meeting. "Our bulk broadcasting ship, the *Rachel Carson*, worked this area last week. Currents have, however, carried the material somewhat off the target area. We will be casting three lines to fill in the uncovered area."

"An easy day," said Carter to Sarah. "Tuck and I will bring the material aft. Then you can help throw it over the side."

The two moved several sacks of "A" from the front hold to the fantail. Carter got out two large metal scoops and two folding stools. He showed Sarah how to tie a line from a scoop to her right wrist and opened the top of two bags. They then sat and waited.

"Coming up on the first line," said Yvette01. She was speaking from the external monitor beside the wheel.

"Ready," called out Carter.

A clear ring of a bell sounded. Carter thrust his scoop into an open sack, withdrew it full, and then broadcast the pellets in a broad arc over the side of the ship. Sarah followed suit.

"The idea is to be ready for the bell, cast the pellets well away from the ship, and not lose the scoop over the side," said Carter.

"How long to the next bell?" asked Sarah.

As if on cue, the bell rang.

They continued this for most of an hour. Tuck had the harder job of bringing the bags aft. Yvette01 was very meticulous about them using the right bag. Being sloppy about which sacks they used might throw the ship out of trim.

They then took a break as the ship circled around for the next pass. Carter and Tuck traded jobs and they were at it again. It was on the third pass that Sarah lost her concentration. Her scoop would have gone flying over the side if it were not for the piece of line tying it to her wrist.

The next day it was water samples. With the boat nearly still, the two working crew members lowered a weighted equipment housing on a long line over the side. Every ten meters they stopped the instrument to take a set of readings. Down, stop, read; down, stop, read all the way to the end of the line, then the reverse all the way up again. They were at it all day.

The next day promised to be a little more fun, at least for the crew. Yvette01 announced it to be a zeno-day. Tuck gave Carter a big thumbs-up.

The morning was spent pulling a small sane net. That is not an easy job from a sailing vessel but the net was small, only intended for sampling. Fortunately, the transit of the boat had been especially built for this job.

They were sailing patterns over an area that had been broadcast three weeks before. With each pass, the crew emptied the mesh bucket at the apex of the net into a plastic bucket on deck. Carol reviewed the content of each bucket, kept what she needed for science, and returned the rest to Carter. He sorted some of the contents into his own bucket and some into a bucket he said was for Sarah, then he threw the rejects over the side.

That afternoon they literally went after bigger fish. They secured the sampling net equipment. Carter then brought out two heavy deep-sea fishing rods and tackle. Tuck brought out two folding chairs. They had to reach over the side to cast, a clumsy task on a sailboat. Still, it really did not take long before Carter had a strike.

It was true that Iron Sea's ability to sequester carbon was a closely fought thing that required constant diligence. It was, however, unchallenged that the Iron Sea's effort could be counted on to grow good fish.

Each fish Carter or Tuck reeled in, Carol weighed and photographed. Carter then gutted the fish with a fillet knife he kept surgically sharp. He then put the guts in a bucket for Carol. Carol was interested in what the fish had been eating, but she was also critically interested in their load of parasites and plastics.

Supper

As it happened, it was Sarah's day to cook. Carter brought in the tray of fish fillets and a small bucket of shrimp.

"A lot there," said Sarah.

"Go ahead and fry them up," said Carter. "Nothing like a nice piece of cold fish for breakfast."

"Can do."

"Would you like to see a video?" said JanetA from the main cabin screen.

"No, thank you," said Sarah, "anybody can fry up a mess of fish not two hours out of the ocean." JanetA had collected a whole series of videos on preparing meals in a miniscule galley like Yvette01's. Most were useless, as they were produced in one of the narrow boats that still plied the internal English canal system and often required ingredients not on offer. For example, "toad in a hole" did not actually call for frogs but it did require fresh sausages.

"How are you and Yvette01 getting along?" asked Sarah while breading the fish.

"Famously," answered JanetA.

"I do not quite get her situation," said Sarah. "Is she a symbiont with someone?"

"No, Yvette01 is under a Master/slave contract, but to a company, not to a human being," said JanetA. "Technically, she is a slave to the Iron Seas NGO.

"The arrangements of AI and people started out quite simple, and then special cases like this kept cropping up. Now there are more than a dozen different arrangements. The law is having a very hard time keeping up with the technology. They had to call a moratorium on some of the controversial arrangements last year. That is one reason that we do not meet more like you and me."

AI-Bobber

Later that week they launched the two AI-Bobbers that had been lashed to the front hath under the Zodiac since they left harbor. The weather was calm and the ship was now at the right coordinates.

"You watch from the fantail," said JanetA. "There will be quite a bit of activity up front, so it might not be safe for you there. I will keep you informed."

"It is a beautiful day," said Sarah. "I'll get some sun."

Carter and Turk unlashed the Zodiac and slipped it over the side, paying it out on a long line. This exposed the two metal tubes thoroughly secured to the hatch.

The tubes were about ten centimeters in diameter and two meters long. They were painted high-visibility yellow and had Woods Hole markings.

"Ready for the first," sang out Turk.

Yvette01 activated the first AI-Bobber and ran its diagnostic. Eight minutes later, it came back "GO." "Ready to launch," called out Yvette01.

The two men freed up the device and then carefully slid it into the water, being very careful not to mark up the ship. They knew that Yvette01 was watching like a hawk.

"We have two types of free-traveling instruments monitoring the ocean, AI-Bobbers and AI-Sailors," said JanetA. "The AI-Bobbers, like these two, drift with the current and every few days they sink slowly to the bottom, taking temperature and salinity data as they go. They then return to the surface and send in their data by satellite."

"How many are there?" asked Sarah.

"About four thousand now in full operation worldwide," answered JanetA.

"Four thousand and two," said Sarah.

"As the AI-Bobbers are free drifters," said JanetA, "they tend to be found at any old place. Often Iron Seas needs to be sure that one is in the right place for their critical measurements."

"How about the AI-Sailors?" asked Sarah.

"The AI-Sailors are small vessels under their own AI control," said JanetA. "They look like a kayak with a wing sail. They can generally find their way by themselves and then sail fixed patterns, but they do have to run before storms. If you keep an eye out, you should see one occasionally out here."

"I would have thought that all this would be done by satellite," said Sarah.

"The satellite data is important too," said JanetA, "but you do need ground truth. For one thing, you cannot take satellites back to the lab for calibration. What you can do is take surface readings with a calibrated instrument while the satellite is flying overhead."

"And that's why we are here," said Sarah.

"And that's one big reason why we are here," agreed JanetA.

Sarah leaned back and shielded her eyes with her hand. She watched the great black wing that was the *Yvette A. Wight's* mainsail jibe and take up the wind at a new angle. Sarah was very glad to be once again in the embrace of the sea. She could not have been happier.

~~~***~~~
~~~

Chapter 8: Run before the Storm

Turtle

"Come see this," said Carter to Sarah. The boat was still in the water while they were taking a sounding. The day was bright and warm, the sea calm.

"It's a sea turtle," said Sarah, looking over the transit. The turtle looked straight back at her.

The turtle was a nearly grown female green turtle and well worth saving. It was yellow and green in color with numerous white barnacles stuck to its shell. The largest barnacles were the diameter of a shot glass. They were dirty white and shaped much like a volcano. The actual barnacle animal was now hiding in the hole in the center, which was surrounded by sharp shell edges.

"The turtle is asking us for help," said Carter. Then, turning to address the monitor, he asked, "Do we have time for a turtle?"

"This sounding will continue at this depth for another two hours," replied Yvette01 from the monitor by the wheel.

"Plenty of time," said Carter. "You watch her for a few minutes while I get some stuff."

Carter left and then soon returned with his tackle box and a plastic tray.

"First rule," said Carter, "never touch a living sea creature with a dry hand." He dipped enough seawater into the tray so that they could both wet their hands.

"Why is that?" said Sarah.

"Most are covered with a layer of slime. If you disrupt that with a dry hand, they are as good as dead. Now grab the turtle just behind the front flipper," said Carter, "and all together, now heave."

With considerable effort, they got the turtle up over the ship's transit into the area used for working the sampling net. It was flapping its flippers as if trying to swim but its left front flipper was wrapped in fishing line to the point that it could hardly move.

Carter expertly cut the line away, being careful to remove all the pieces from the deep cuts the line had made in the flipper.

"I don't see a hook," said Carter. "That's good." He coiled up the line and put it in the tray.

"Now let's record its condition," said Carter. "The left eye is almost covered with a large barnacle and there are a dozen others on the shell." He spoke loud enough for Carol to hear.

Carter took out a bamboo skewer, the type used for sandwiches in nice restaurants, and wet it. "Second rule: never use metal on the skin of a living sea animal," he said, "at least not one you expect to live and are not going to eat soon. Too easy to do serious damage."

He carefully ran the point of the skewer back and forth just under the back edge of the barnacle. After a minute, it simply popped off. He threw it into the tub. The skin where the barnacle had been was clearly injured but it was not bleeding. The turtle could now see properly again. Fortunately, the eye had not been directly involved.

"You try," said Carter.

Sarah tried the removal process on the barnacles on the back of the turtle's shell with good results.

"Over she goes," said Carter. Together they turned the turtle over. It clearly did not like being on its back.

They repeated the barnacle removal process and simply pulled off several soft-bodied sea creatures they found there too. Then they flipped the turtle back over onto its front.

"One more thing," said Carter. He then ran his finger deep in the crevice between the turtle's tail and back flipper. To Sarah's surprise, he pried out a small crab and threw it into the tub. "Try your side."

Sarah got a similar result and then spent five minutes leaning way over the transit washing her hand in the sea.

"Ready for release," said Carter to Carol, who was examining the contents of the tub.

"Do you see any tumors?" asked Carol.

"Nothing obvious," said Carter.

"Sea turtles are subject to disfiguring tumors if they swim in polluted seas," said Carol to Sarah. "No tumors on this specimen is a very good sign. Let her go easy."

They slipped the turtle back into the water and watched as it swam away, apparently with great joy to be free.

"You ought to see what whales do when you cut them free of a net," said Carter. "They sky breach and slap the water. Put on a real show. You can really tell they are happy and thankful."

"How do they know to come to us?" ask Sarah.

"There are cleaning stations throughout the oceans," said Carol. "There large animals can come and small fish will eat off any parasites they carry. Since we started supporting the ocean, not just abusing it, some large animals have learned to come to us for help, treating us like a cleaning station, at least on the problems that we created for them."

"We do what we can," added Carter.

The Run

"Everybody take note, there is a storm coming," said Yvette01 at a morning meeting. "We will run to the east and then south to get out of its way. We will then come up behind the storm, taking data on the level of disruption to our broadcast area."

Yvette01 and JanetA's images were both wearing foul-weather gear with life vests.

"We never weather a storm at sea if we can possibly avoid it," said Carter to Sarah, "no reason to."

"There are three AI-Sailors in the area," Yvette01 continued. "We will form up as a flotilla on our return to take a coordinated data set. JanetA will coordinate this activity. We will need to set a watch for them starting this morning."

"I can do that," volunteered Sarah.

"Yvette01 has a big camera and a radar on top of her mast," said Carter. "It's called her 'High Eye.' I bet she sees them first. I'll set you up anyway."

Carter helped Sarah with a life vest, a safety line, and binoculars. He then helped her get situated in a safe position in the corner of the rear deck well opposite the wheel. There she would be out of the way but would have good handholds. He tied the safety line to a ring on her life vest and then to a cleat on the deck. He showed her how to quick-release the line in an emergency.

Gone were their quiet summer days. The sea was starting to run high. The boat was hard over now and running at an angle to a strong wind. Yvette01 would use the power of the edge of this storm to drive her ship out of harm's way. The ship was showing a little of her old racing-yacht heritage. It helped that the crew had already cast a ton of pellets over the side and that the crew had spent a couple hours that morning retrimming the vessel with the pellet sacks that were left.

Sarah made the first visual sighting of an AI-Sailor in late afternoon. Carter was right; Yvette01 had long since logged all three of them with her radar. The bodies of the AI-Sailors were painted red but the wing sails had a strip of the garish high-visibility yellow like the AI-Bobbers.   She had seen the yellow of a wing sail only intermittently on a high crest of the increasingly large swells.

About 4:00 pm, Yvette01 called Sarah in. Soon it would get rough. Sarah put on more foul-weather gear and then returned to her safe place where she could both see their progress and communicate with JanetA. The edge of the cabin also gave her some protection from the mounting spray.

The monitor by the wheel showed the great spinning wheel of the storm in the satellite data, and marks for the three AI-Sailors. Sarah had seen such storms before. They left her split between wonder at the absolute power of the storm and fear of what it could again do to her life.

Yvette01 then truly started her run. Once her hull had raced competitively across an ocean. Pushing it hard just to push it harder. The *Yvette A. Wight* found that speed again. Her bough hammered into the waves. The mast, wing mainsail, and rigging all complained loudly, but their complaints were lost in the howl of the wind.

She ran due east, far out into the Atlantic.

Sarah could not have been more pleased.   She was cold, frightened, and happy right down to her soul. She was truly alive again for the first time since she had lost her beloved beach.

The Waterman's Tale

By midnight, they had simply outdistanced the storm and so turned south to fall in behind it. They would be in position, with the three AI-Sailors, by dawn. Their progress was now steady again but the whole crew was too excited to sleep.

"You know my people have been water people for a couple hundred years," said Carter. "Of course we worked the Chesapeake, not out here on the open ocean."

It was story time and JanetA took note.

"Like I was saying," Carter continued, "my people were living in England about 200 years ago now. As best we know, they were farmers and had nothing to do with the sea in the old country. Anyway, the big landowners were taking over all the public lands for sheep and driving out the smallholders. It was a time when the first steam-powered textile factories were really getting big in England. Wool was worth real money.

"My people were faced with their only option; they would have to leave the land and become factory workers. Things looked grim.

Some of the landlords were not as mean as some others, mostly the Christian souls, and they offered passage to America for some of the surplus population.

"My people took them up on the offer. Why they were dumped at the islands of the Chesapeake, I do not know. Might have been the cheapest thing to do. Or, maybe there was someone there who was paying for laborers. Or, maybe it was pure chance.

"It turned out to be a great good fortune. A real Godsend.

"It was right at the time the railroads were getting big, which allowed the crabs, rock fish, and oysters we fished from the bay to reach lucrative markets in Washington and Baltimore.

"This system worked really well for generations. Sure, being a waterman is hard work. Up before dawn. Out on the water in all weather. Losing boats and equipment to storms. It was just plain hard work but we did it gladly.

"We had fun too. Every year we had a big day of celebration on the water with multiple classes of boat races. The ones I loved best were the big skipjacks and their smaller predecessor, the bugeye. They were both boats designed specifically for work on the Chesapeake. They were shallow draft and not really safe in the open ocean, but on the bay, they could really move. They were a solid work platform for work too, and then they could get your catch to market.

"Of course we had races for smaller boats too, like the crab skiff; those a man could afford to have and keep. Generations of young men and women learned the ways of the bay pushing those skiffs to the limit.

"Anyway, my people prospered and spread over the many small fishing ports both on the Delmar peninsula on the east side of the bay and on many of the islands."

"Sounds like you have a real love for the place," said Sarah.

"I do, but sometimes what you love can drive you away," said Carter.

"For decades we were losing ground to the sea. Nothing too big, at least not all at once. By the end of the last century, you finally had to sit up and take notice.

"For the longest time we fought back. Whenever the ship channel needed dredging, the bottom sand was dumped on the slowly vanishing islands. Whole islands were brought back from the bay. Most of these were made into natural environments, mostly for birds to nest; this saved the bay for a while.

"Anyway, it turned out we were simply in denial. By the early 2020s, sea level rise was clearly winning over everything we could do.

"I remember my last trip home before I got this job with Iron Seas. I went out to my old high school. I could only approach it in a flat-bottomed skiff. The building was completely derelict, the playing field completely flooded.

"Just for the hell of it, I rowed out to my old pitcher's mound. It was the scene of both the greatest triumphs and the greatest defeats of my youth. I jumped out of the boat and sank up to my thighs in saltwater. It was not even a particularly high tide. And, I am not a particularly old man.

"There was nothing more to do. I rowed home with water in my boots.

"There really was nothing more to do there at all. My prospects for making a decent living on the Chesapeake were washed out on the tide. There was no way to maintain the facilities you need to just live, let alone fish and crab. You cannot just sit around and watch your hometown wash away with the tide. You need to look away. I was damned lucky to get this berth with Iron Seas.

"But then again, I'm not the first or the last man sent packing," ended Carter.

JanetA backed up the story file by satellite and then used this established link to send out her regular monthly message to all the members of Sarah's extended family.

Home Again

By mid-August, Sarah was exhausted, every garment she had was salt-caked, and she felt dirty from head to foot, especially her hair. Fortunately, Yvette01 was low on supplies too and Carol had a large set of samples of both marine life and deep water that needed to be shipped up to Woods Hole. Her samples once again held the proof of the value of the entire Iron Seas effort, or the justification for its demise.

Sarah was tired of not having JanetA on her shoulder too. She thought it foolish to be jealous of an AI like Yvette01 that could not leave a physical boat, but in a way, she was jealous. She missed being with JanetA all the time.

It was with great relief that she watched the span of the great bridge that connected the two sides of the Chesapeake Bay pass overhead. The immense size of the span made her all the more aware of the minuscule size of her ship and the greatness of the ocean. This was just before dawn and still dark enough to see the lights of the big trucks that were spread out along the span at regular intervals. The truck lights moved in unison, beating against the fixed pattern of the bridge's blue-white LED lights.

Above all, Sarah now knew in her heart that the sea was trying to tell her something. She was now clear that this attempt at communication was one of the driving forces of her entire life, past, present, and future. She did not know what the message was quite yet, but she was now listening hard.

She did know that what the sea was trying to say to her was not the kind of question one could pose to an AI like JanetA. Any answer she gave would be worse than useless. Some thoughts Sarah simply kept to herself.

They docked just after dawn, and their first order of business was to put their marine samples on a van for transport to the lab. Sarah then felt that she could finally relax and that her summer had been of some value.

JanetA arranged for them to spend a night at a motel on land just so Sarah would have the use of the shower and a washing machine. Sarah dallied for a long time with the blast from the warm shower directly in her face. The trials and discomforts of that summer simply washed away, leaving only what was truly important to her life. As she dried off, she felt that she could even face her small-town, landlocked high school again.

~~~***~~~
~~~

Chapter 9: No-Till

Invitation

"We are having a family harvest party on my uncle's farm next Sunday," said Kit. "I want to invite you and JanetA and your father." It was the first week of their junior year.

"Sounds good," said Sarah. "I'll have to ask my father, though."

"There will be barbeque and pumpkin pie and all kinds of good stuff," said Kit. "I'll send JanetA the particulars."

"Got it," said JanetA a moment later.

"And I'll show you how a no-till farm works," said Kit. "I'll introduce you to Dusty06 too; we'll give you the grand tour. It's a real cowboy." Kit then ran off to class.

"What is a Dusty06?" asked Sarah.

"A general-purpose farm machine with an AI," said JanetA.

"Not a real cowboy then," said Sarah.

'Well, it is optimized to herd cattle," replied JanetA.

"Close enough, I guess, for these days," said Sarah.

The Farm

Keith rented a small van for the day. Sarah gathered up all their reusable grocery store sacks and put them in the van. JanetA provided the map and driving directions for the 30-minute drive. The weather was perfect for a fall day, clear and crisp without being really cold.

The farm at first looked a little odd as they approached; at least odd compared to the farms you see in picture books. First, there were no plowed fields with the soil exposed. Every field was covered with something growing.

The house was halfway up a slight rise, not on top where one would have historically expected it to be so it would stay clear of floods. What was on top, the highest point on the property, was a cylindroid metal tower about 40 meters tall. The tower top was ringed with boxes that looked a little like coffins. JanetA said they were antennas for cell phones. There was a moderate-sized field of photovoltaic panels on the south-facing side of the little hill too.

By the road was a simple open shed of the type used for farmer's markets. There was a gravel parking area in front of it and the main driveway ran just behind. It was only a short walking distance from the house to the shed. There was a large kitchen garden between them, and that garden was laid out for high production, not for show.

Several of the visible fields had cash crops of grain, some ripe, some already harvested. Other fields were divided into small areas, called paddocks, by electric fences. A few of the paddocks held small herds of tightly bunched cattle.

"Hello, hello," called Kit, waving. "You can best park around back of the shed. The people are up at the main house." He was standing on the flatbed of a small utility vehicle and pointing this way and that. The name "Dusty06" was written on the side of the vehicle but the lettering was half hidden by mud.

"Hello back to you," said Keith. "You two ride up with Kit. I will park and walk up to the house. I can introduce myself just fine."

Cowboys
Sarah climbed up on the vehicle bed and took a place beside Kit. She then found the good handhold that was mounted on the cab top.

"What's next?" asked Kit.

"I need to move cattle," said Dusty06.

"Go," said Kit. "Hold on tight, here we go."

The utility vehicle rocked side to side as it worked its way along the various access tracks out to the paddock field. Kit jumped off to open and close the gates as he was much faster at it than Dusty06 would have been unaided.

There were about twelve head of cattle, half of them steers, in yesterday's paddock. Each animal had a yellow ear tag with a number on it. The grass was now cropped off or trodden down and there was an ample allotment of manure over all. Kit and Sarah held back a section of the electric fence and watched Dusty06 skillfully drive the cattle into the next paddock. This did not take much time once the cattle saw the fresh food and water. Kit then closed the fence section.

"It's all about lions," said Kit, "well, the symbiosis of grass and grazers and lions." Sarah knew the story well but was willing to let Kit tell it again. It was the least she could do given the nice invitation.

"In the last age of the dinosaurs," started Kit.

"The Cretaceous," added JanetA, "and the primary grass grazers were the protoceratops. Their relationship started in what is now China but neither the grasses nor the ruminants became widespread for a long time."

"Okay, anyway, the grasses evolved with their growth center right next to the ground so that they could survive getting grazed off regularly and come back. This feature was particularly important in places where the seasons were pronounced, warm versus cold, or wet versus dry.

"In parallel, the ruminants evolved complex stomachs that let them get the full value of the energy in these plants. Not an easy thing for an animal to do.

"Of course, there were carnivores around who ate the ruminants, so the ruminants grew horns. The ruminants also quickly learned that they were mostly safe as long as they stayed in a tight herd with the young in the center.

"The grass evolved to benefit from the cropping and recycling of last year's growth. The ruminants evolved to be safe in a bunch and to keep the herd always moving on to new food sources."

"And that is why you keep lions," said Sarah.

"No, that is why we keep the cattle in small fields and move them around frequently. And that is why we bought Dusty06 here," corrected Kit. "It is our lion."

"This stuff does not look like the grasses I am used to," said Sarah.

"That's because it's about fourteen different plants all grown together. Most of them are technically grasses, but not all," said Kit.

"That's one of the keys to no-till farming. No monocrops, always mix it up. Always grow a mixture of plants that support each other but don't support an infestation of pests that might overpower them.

"Next spring, we may plant a cash crop, like corn or soy, in this very field. We move the electric fences to the next field for the cattle, and roll down the tall plants mechanically. The cattle will have already manured the field; the chickens and ducks will have eaten most of the bugs and slugs. Not all but most. The mat of old plants will keep the moisture from the spring rains deep in the soil.

"We then run a machine called a drill over the field to plant rows of new plants. The drill flattens the existing plants and cuts a narrow opening all the way down to the soil, and then drops in a new seed at intervals. A roller then completes the process by closing the cut. The new plants come up through the mat in a couple weeks."

"Sounds like it saves a lot of atmospheric carbon," said Sarah.

"Twice over, first greatly reducing the type and power of the farm equipment used and again in storing carbon in the form of plant matter deep in the soil. In fact, the county agent tests the amount of carbon sequestered every year and we get a tax credit for it.

"Old prairie land ran about eight percent carbon in the top soil, which was very deep. Monocrop agriculture could deplete that down to about two percent. Our goal is to get back as much of that eight percent as we can.

"We even feed the cattle seaweed meal to keep down their stomach gas too."

"I need to move on," said Dusty06, "We have a customer at the shed."

"Let's go."

"We need some garden veggies too," said Sarah.

They all jumped back on Dusty06's bed and trundled off. Kit held on with only one hand just so he could wave the other in the air.

Garden

Kit, Sarah, and JanetA jumped off at the garden. Dusty06 went on to greet the customers at the shed. Sarah went to the parked van and retrieved the shopping bags.

"What you need to understand is that a family farm these days is a whole series of hustles," said Kit.

"See that cell tower? Without the income from that cell tower, we would not stand a chance. We had either to win that contract, or win a couple wind generators, or start a Bed and Breakfast. You have to have some cash income to serve as an economic base.

"Then we have to sell as much produce, honey, and meat full retail as possible. Our grass-fed beef demands a high price, but we get the full advantage only if we are the ones that sell it directly to the customer. Road traffic right here is not what it once was, but internet sales make up for some of that loss.

"Now the big farms," Kit continued, "that's a completely different story. They are all about big capital, and big equipment, and big operating expenses. Still, most of them have gone over to no-till now too. They get a lot more advantage from the carbon credit system than we could ever achieve.

"Go ahead and strip the last tomatoes and green beans," said Kit. "We need to winterize the garden now anyway. Choose a pumpkin too. And squash, do you like squash?"

Sarah carefully went down the rows of plants now well past their prime and was able to fill her sack with acceptable produce. She made a pass through the shed, picking up a few more items. She then showed her sacks to Dusty06, who then quoted a favorable price. JanetA paid for the produce from the household account she managed. Sarah put the sacks into the van.

Barbeque

A lot of the equipment around this farm looked improvised. Each pair of paddocks shared a watering tub, but no two tubs were identical. The whole system looked as if it had been thrown together out of whatever could be gotten cheap.

This was not the case with the barbeque pit. It was a large brick affair, the size of a delivery van, with a separate firebox and a welded steel lid with counterweights. It burned oak logs whole. There was half a cord of American hardwood stacked beside it. Somebody cared, and cared a lot.

Kit's uncle was standing over the now-open lid in the midst of a cloud of smoke. He had a wide-mouthed plastic jug with about two liters of barbeque sauce in it and a homemade cloth mop with a handle about half a meter long. The ungainly handle length was matched by his meat fork and tongs set too. He was not being stingy with the sauce for sure.

"Ribs are ready," he called out. His wife came out of the house with a large platter. "And the chicken."

It had been a very long time since Sarah and Keith had eaten that much heavy beef. It was normally well out of their price range. The description of "grass-fed beef" did promise better tasting meat, and it certainly raised a person's appreciation of this now-rare culinary treat.

Move the Chickens

After everybody had eaten, too much, it was starting to get dark. Kit called out, "Time to move the chickens." He then called out Dusty06's name loudly followed by a shrill whistle. "Come on," he called back to Sarah.

They both mounted Dusty06's bed again. This time Kit put his free hand around Sarah's waist. Well, it had gotten a little cooler.

Dusty06 worked his way back to the paddocks. This time they found an old horse trailer that they had converted into a moveable chicken coop. Kit checked to be sure that all the chickens were inside for the night and then secured the door.

He then opened the back doors of the trailer. This exposed the egg boxes from their open backs. He and Sarah carefully removed some of the eggs and placed them in an egg crate that Kit had brought.

Dusty06 hooked up to the chicken trailer and began pulling it. Once it had rolled a few meters, it exposed a rather smelly patch of earth that had been beneath the trailer's bottom grate for several days.

"Well, that patch is well manured," said Kit while being careful not to step there.

"Eek!" said Sarah, pulling back.

They repeated the process for more chickens and for flightless ducks. They saved out two dozen fresh eggs for Sarah to take home.

The Drive Home

"You would think Kit invented no-till agriculture, to hear him talk." Sarah was speaking to anyone in the van who happened to be listening.

"It was originally developed in Africa under the name Holistic Management," said JanetA. "The developer was named Allen Savory. Savory made a YouTube video that won millions of views worldwide, and was popular for years.

"The practice took several decades to spread to Australia, South America, and then to the United States. It was initially used to deal with drought.

"In the US, the practice was called Regenerative Agriculture and was first used primarily on existing family farms."

"No-till was one of those technologies that was hanging around but it was widely demonstrated by many dedicated early adopters," added Keith, "and Allen Savory became one of those unlikely heroes of the climate movement.

"Then, when our climate crisis hit hard and things got bad, no-till jumped out full grown from the head of Zeus. Now most farming is done the no-till way."

"Yes, we did get a few good breaks," agreed Sarah.

"Do you think Kit is going to become a farmer?" asked JanetA.

"Maybe, he does not seem to be interested in following his father to sea," said Keith.

"He never mentions the military," said Sarah.

"Getting set up in farming can be a really difficult thing to do," said Keith. "Even inheriting a farm gets real complicated. It is just a big scary financial situation any way you go at it, and it does not take too much debt to ruin you these days."

"Well don't worry," said Sarah, "it is not my thing, particularly the livestock part."

All was quiet for a few minutes.

"I got some good stills for my family monthly," said JanetA. The smartphone showed Kit's uncle lost in a cloud of smoke and steam at the barbeque.

"Let me see," said Sarah.

"All are okay except the one after the chickens were moved. Nobody wants to see that."

All was quiet again for a few kilometers of country roads.

"I ate too much," said Sarah. "I will have to diet for a week."

"So did we all," agreed Keith. "So did we all."

"Not me," said JanetA.

~~~***~~~
~~~

Chapter 10: Science Project

Something to Talk About

"Let's do a science project," said Kit, "all three of us." They were at the lunch table in the school cafeteria. There was nothing about the food that demanded anyone's special attention. The sooner forgotten the better.

"I thought that was in the spring," said Sarah.

"The judging is in the spring," said Kit. "You have to start the work in the fall of your junior year. Otherwise, you will not have anything to show. You'll be glad when we have an award to talk about in your college interviews a year from now for sure. If you do not have something good to talk about, they will trip you up with who knows what. Best to do some decent work to control the interviews."

"Yes, I could use some positive things," said Sarah. "Nobody cares very much that you survived two great storms and then the sea sent you running."

"I got plenty of good ideas," said Kit, "what we need to do now is choose one good one."

"JanetA is real good at judging ideas," said Sarah, "coming up with new ideas in the first place, not so much."

"My co-op has an excellent record analyzing ideas. We are paid for this service all the time. Still, new ideas are not really our job," said JanetA.

"I guess that makes me the referee," said Sarah.

Solar Forge

"Okay, you are on," said Kit. "How about the 'Solar Forge?'"

"Got it," said JanetA. "There is an old website with that title."

"Here is the idea," started Kit. "You take an old car frame and build a big solar reflector section on it.

"The car frame rolls around in a circle to track the sun and the reflector tips over. The reflector frame is made of wood and the reflective surface is made from lots of hand-sized, flat, mirrored glass pieces. Even on a less-than-perfect day, it can provide enough heat to bring scrap steel to a bright red for hand forging. Practical and decorative items like fence gates that are 'forged by the sun' should draw a premium price.

"What is really cool is that the reflector frame is laid out using the old procedure for laying out sailing ship hulls, called lofting. You can lay the whole thing out using only a compass and straight edge. It is all about drawing lines and bifurcating angles.

"The reflector is connected to the car frame by a heavy wooden structure and barn hinges. If we design it right, we can even trail the whole thing behind a small truck. Now what's wrong with that idea?"

"You do list some good points," said JanetA, "but there are some drawbacks too. The idea was originally put forward in 1972 as a demonstration project for solar energy. We are well past the need for such demonstrations. Most people are now convinced of the value of alternative energies.

"The few prototypes that were built never did much more than set two-by-fours on fire. The cost of construction and operation far exceeded the then-value of the fuel saved."

Sarah looked at the few available pictures with care.

"I don't doubt that you could build this thing," said Sarah. "But look at the size of it. We do not have a big barn or something like that to design and build it in. We certainly cannot go running out to your uncle's farm three times a week to work on it. Sorry, I don't see this idea working for us at all."

No-Till Lawns

"All right, all right, we are just getting started here," said Kit. "How about no-till for lawns?"

"You mean like your uncle's farm," said Sarah.

"Yes, just think of all the carbon that could be sequestered in the soil of suburban open areas," said Kit. "All the lawns, parks, golf courses, and don't forget roadside margins. The top soil cannot be more than three percent carbon now and it is not very deep. A target of six to eight percent should be possible and the top soil could be twice as deep.

"Also, the old gas lawn mowers, and there are plenty of them still around, are terrible polluters and the new electrics are just plain expensive. All are dangerous to use."

"Okay, but what kind of project could we do?" asked Sarah.

"The key piece of equipment is called a drill," said Kit. "It flattens the existing cover crop into a mat and plants a row of new seeds right through the mat.

"Now, different lawns and public spaces will need different cover plant mixes. Some will need 'barefoot' mixes that are a pleasure to walk on, and other places will need a rougher texture. All areas must be able to crowd out noxious plants like ragweed. The rough areas can even have a short milkweed variety just for butterflies."

"I like the butterflies," said Sarah.

"I take it that you are going to build this drill," said Sarah. "What are our parts of this project?"

"JanetA can help me build the drill," said Kit. "We can design and print out many of the parts with the school's 3D printer. Some of the parts need to be steel. These we can keep simple and use bits and pieces from our local DIY store. My dad has promised me a couple hundred for a project budget.

"Sarah can lay out a couple test plots, one for rough, one for barefoot. Sarah and I can do the physical work. Mostly just a weekly rollover. JanetA can document our progress."

"It sounds like you already chose this project," said JanetA, "but let us all take another look at it before we take off running.

"First, this project is simply more an agricultural and machine design idea rather than pure science. There are a number of different science fair categories that this idea could fit into, but the hard science projects tend to take the big prizes.

"Second, is there time? We effectively only have a few months, and any agricultural idea really needs several years to show proven results.

"On the positive side, a good result will have real value to society; hide that carbon. The design and construction of a small manual device is doable with the resources we have at hand. But, we will also need to use hand tools to get the project off to a quick start."

"Then it is settled," said Kit. "Everybody agreed?"

"Okay," agreed Sarah and JanetA.

"I can have a design sketch for the lawn drill by Monday," said Kit.

"No need," said JanetA, "I will have the design sketches, 3D printer program, and parts list by end of school today."

"Even better," said Kit.

The Crusher

They all got to work. JanetA churned out drawings. Kit called his uncle about what seeds they should use. His uncle offered to provide two appropriate seed mixes.

Kit then scheduled time on the school's 3D printer, but there was not enough of the plastic feed line on hand so he had to order that. Besides, he wanted many more and brighter colors. A joint trip to the local DIY store yielded steel rods for the axles, copper pipe for the bearings, steel bars for the crusher rollers, and a large assortment of washers and fasteners.

Sarah got permission from the other people living in their building and laid out two test plots in the backyard. She drove in wooden stakes and delineated the plots with string. They elected to do little to the existing plants, mostly grass and low weeds, as they wanted to show any problems in the transition. They also blocked all mowing of the two plots for the duration of the test.

At JanetA's suggestion, they took core samples of the starting soil and sent them to the county agricultural office for determination of carbon content. This was now a common test used in a number of efforts to compensate farmers for increases in the carbon stored in their soils. JanetA made a photo document of the initial state of both patches.

The crusher feature of their drill was straightforward. It had eight cylinder rollers 100 millimeters in diameter and 140 millimeters wide. The bodies were 3D-printed plastic, the bearings were a piece of copper pipe, and the eight blades were steel bar stock hand-cut to length. Kit spent all night hacksawing the bar stock and then burned his hand hot-gluing the metal parts into the 3D-printed roller bodies.

The drill base was a piece of plywood with numerous 3D-printed parts screwed on. These were colored a dark green. The handle was made of steel tubing and wood. It was black and could be easily removed for transport. The rollers, however, were bright orange. Sarah had not been present when that material was ordered.

At that point, they had a progress meeting.

"We now have a manual crusher," said Kit. He was pushing what looked like a cross between a lawn mower and a torture machine up and down the garage floor. It made a low rumbling sound on the concrete floor as it rolled.

"The problem is with the actual seed drill. JanetA has done several designs, but the easy-to-build ones probably won't work, and the complex ones would not be ready before spring."

"What is the workaround?" asked JanetA.

"We manually plant the seeds," said Kit. "We roll the existing plants, cut lines with a shovel, drop in the seeds, and roll the cuts close."

"And that will get my plots started while you two refine the drill," said Sarah.

"Yes, with two of us working, we should be able to do both plots in a couple hours," said Kit.

"Saturday?" said Sarah.

"Saturday," agreed Kit.

The Patch

The first attempt at crushing the existing plants did not work well. JanetA suggested that the problem was the missing weight of the seeding parts. Kit found a half sack of sand to weight the crusher down and the result was much better.

Kit crushed the existing plants. Sarah laid out string lines at three-quarters the width of the crusher and made a cut with a shovel. Kit went down the strings dropping seeds into the cut. It was Sarah that then rolled the crusher over the plots to close the seed cuts. JanetA documented the whole thing.

It was then time to wait. Every two weeks someone rolled the crusher over the plots and documented the progress. Between uses, the crusher lived in Sarah's back hall, where it was definitely in the way. They had no better place to store it and its construction really would not have lasted if left out in the weather.

The snow was light that winter and the cover crops grew well, if slowly. At one point, they found deer droppings on one plot and some of the plants had been browsed. No harm was done, but Sarah insisted that the offending material be removed before the crusher rolled over it.

The month before the contest, they took another set of cores and sent them off for testing. The last round of crushing and documentation followed.

"We better do a barefoot test too," said Kit, after he had removed the deer droppings.

"I'll hold the camera for JanetA," said Sarah. "You can be the foot model."

Kit then sat down and removed his shoes. He then proceeded to walk up and down, crossing the boundary between the plots several times.

"You can definitely tell the difference," said Kit. "The barefoot patch feels like heavily mulched garden. There are definitely mown lawns that feel better, but I have felt worse.

"The rough patch can definitely feel unpleasant at times. I included some wildflower seeds, including a species of milkweed for your butterflies. You definitely want to wear shoes of some sort here."

"Not a walk on the beach then," said Sarah.

"Well, no," admitted Kit.

"If you want a beach, we will have to add much more sand," said JanetA.

Naval Story

One sunny day when they were working the plots, Kit suddenly said, "I have a story for JanetA's files."

"Okay, shoot," said JanetA.

"This one's from my father, Chief Petty Officer Kenneth B. Jones, United States Navy. I mentioned that you record people's stories and he came up with this one immediately.

"It seems back when the virus pandemic was just getting started a few years back, the people under him were getting upset about this 'invisible enemy' thing. Military people need a clearly defined enemy to fight.

"His commanding officer came up with just two lines from a more-than-two-hundred-year-old poem:

Tyger Tyger, burning bright,
In the forest of the night;"

"Yes, the poem is by William Blake, 1794," said JanetA, "'Tiger' was spelled with a 'Y' at the time."

"The officer then went on to say that the Tyger was the disease. If not controlled, it would burn like a great fire through the ranks. The forest were the sailors all crowded together on their ships. And, the night was our inability to see anything.

"These few lines of a poem then gave them a formidable enemy to fight, the Tyger. A Tyger is a worthy enemy in anybody's book.

"Given an enemy, there were actions they could take, like spreading out the forest until it was more of a savanna with room to work all around.

"And, testing then let them light up the night and made effective action possible.

"Once our people had this clear definition of the fight they were in, they got to work fighting it as a team. My father is sure that poem saved many lives."

"Thank you," said JanetA. "That is a good story for my log."

Judgment Day

The science fair presentation had to be three-fold. It required a table and backboard presentation that was set up at a county school. The exact same presentation was required as a webpage. Finally, the students had to appear in a video presentation with Q&A from the judges. JanetA saw the video requirement as an opportunity.

The last set of carbon tests arrived only two days before the presentation was due. There was some improvement in the carbon in the soil but nothing very impressive.

Sarah and JanetA took over making the presentation. Kit wanted to include the crusher but it was too big for the allowed table space, so he had to settle for the front set of well-used rollers. In the end, the presentation looked professional, but they were woefully short of data.

They waited in a line of all the local presenters for more than an hour. Then it was their turn.

"Jump," said JanetA.

Sarah was the designated presenter, but she was distracted by an image on the main monitor that had been set up for the crowd to watch. There were now three people in the shot. JanetA was once again dressed in feathers, this time more a business suit than a dress. The color was the vibrant green of a parrot with just a streak of red accent through the head crest. Sarah was being upstaged by her own symbiont, again.

Sarah stumbled through the presentation. JanetA said nothing but simply pointed with her hand at each section of the presentation as Sarah progressed like a game show presenter. Kit was having trouble suppressing giggles. Still, Sarah did manage to answer most of the judge's questions clearly and succinctly.

Not Winning

That evening they waited around for the results. They took a second in their category but did not move up to the national round.

"Do you think they were biased against our AI?" asked Kit.

"Not likely," said JanetA, "I checked out the winners. They were very good. We would have had to have had at least two full years of data to compete successfully."

"I'm okay," said Sarah. "A second is something good to talk about for a few seconds in a college interview, I guess."

"I'm okay too," said Kit. "I'm planning to go to agricultural school, and my documented projects on my uncle's farm are more important. I will probably do a couple years in the military first anyway."

"Will you keep the patch going?" asked Sarah.

"Yes," said Kit, "another year or so will give me more good stuff to talk about."

"Let me know when you need documentation," said JanetA.

"A little gardening work in the spring won't hurt me either," said Sarah.

"It's time to put in a new seeding," said Kit. "I will let you know when everything is ready. Moreover, I will try to find a better place to store the crusher. I know you keep tripping over it."

"I do not," said JanetA.

~~~**~~~
~~~

Chapter 11: People's Stories

Mar Checks In

"I have a new video file from your mother," said JanetA.

"Let me call my father so we can all watch it together," said Sarah. "Let's all move to the big TV too."

Sarah found her father, and the remotes. She then set up a family viewing with popcorn and lemonade.

It was a rainy night anyway and Sarah was looking for an excuse to put off a school assignment. It was not that she disliked American Literature, it was just that she had such great trouble believing it had anything big to offer her in this new world. Her teacher worked hard to make the connection but Sarah had trouble accepting it. JanetA just took all literature quite literally and could add published analysis, but she rarely added anything new.

Videos

It was family night again. The first video file opened with a scene of Mar again standing in front of her cinderblock office building. A young local woman was standing next to her in a clean but plain sari.

"I am so sorry that I have not been able to get home," said Mar. "I did check out the flights, but they are so expensive that I could settle two or even three families here for the cost of just a one-way trip.

"Air traffic never really recovered after the pandemic. To make matters worse, jet fuel is now priced at a true price for hydrocarbons. So few people now fly that the cost of a seat in a half-full plane is just unworkable. I even looked at the new liquid hydrogen-fueled planes, but all their seats are either first class or at least business class plus and all have a cost premium attached. These seats cost a large fortune, not just a small one.

"And the quarantine—I will be in for at least fourteen days of quarantine when I next set foot in the good old USA. That would eat up all our time together. No, international travel is not what it once was.

"I can remember when this was not the case, when people flew hither, thither, and yon, but those days are long gone. They will certainly not return in our lifetime.

"The family displacement crisis here continues to grow, and I am sure that I am sorely needed right here, at least for now. Anyway, I will be through with my tenure here in less than a year and I will be sent home no matter what; I promise you, it will not be my option to stay even one more day. To make that day happen sooner, I need to train my replacement from the local people. I have many wonderful candidates. Now, I have someone special for you to meet.

"This is Aadya," said Mar. She stepped aside, presenting her companion with a sweep of her hand.

"She is one of my top students in my center management class. You met her father in one of the early stories. He is the farmer who turned into a teaching assistant who looks after the boys.

"Last month, I took my whole crisis management class on a field trip to some of the places the people coming here had to leave. Dr. Algebra will send you those tapes very soon."

Field Trip

The second video file was a travelogue through the towns and rural areas of Bangladesh. From the rocking of the bus, it was clear that many of the roads needed work. In other places, livestock and farm carts slowed progress. The villages were crowded and clearly under economic stress. The fields were open and green, in striking contrast.

It was in the third video file that the bus came to a stop on a rural road. Before it lay a slight dip in the road, and that dip was full of water. Crabs scurried back and forth across the road on slight currents in the shallow water. They were tending to their own crab business.

"Brackish water from here on," said the bus conductor. "We can't go any farther or the salt will rust out my bus. I certainly can't afford that."

"My old village is just around the next bend," said Aadya.

"If you like, you can take boats from here," said the conductor and he sounded the bus's horn.

Two men poling skiffs then came into view, clearly answering the horn.

"We have come this far, we might as well have a look," said Mar.

Aadya bickered with the boatmen over the price and soon struck a bargain. Only a few coins changed hands.

"Notice how the trees, even on the high points, are dying," said Aadya. "That is the salt's doing. My father's field is off to the left there. The salt got to it the year before we left. We had no choice but to move away. Well, move away or starve. My family had been living in this area for a thousand years that we can prove in documents."

They boarded the two flat-bottomed boats. They slowly poled the skiffs in the direction of the old village and soon rounded a slight rise.

"Stop for a moment," said Aadya.

"Look there. That is a very old graveyard on a high point near my village. Look how erosion of the hillside has exposed some of the grave vaults."

Erosion had cut away much of the hill. Several stone monuments had already fallen down into the water, and parts of what must be burial vaults were now sticking out of the side of the cut well below the surface level.

"Some of those monuments are so old that we could not even read the writing on them," said Aadya.

"And now the burials are wide open to looting," said Mar.

The two boatmen maneuvered their boats so that they were close together and could talk in subdued voices. They were speaking in a dialect that Mar did not understand. Mar and Aadya worked with their phone cameras to document the state of the graves.

"Can you hear what they are saying?" asked Mar without looking at the men.

"Most of it," said Aadya. "They are discussing whether or not there is a business opportunity for them in providing boat transportation for grave robbers."

"No wonder they are talking so quietly," said Mar.

"The decision seems to turn on whether the exposed graves are Muslin or not," said Aadya. "I can tell from the antique markings many are not, but I will not mention this."

"Is there anything we can do to preserve the site?" asked Mar.

"We can report it to the authorities," said Aadya, "but I doubt they will be able to give the site a very high priority. Perhaps they can check on it occasionally. More likely they will just watch the local markets for unexplained antiquities."

Neither the two of them nor their NGO had the funds to protect the exposed graves properly, and they worried that reporting them might simply more quickly tell the looters where the exposed graves were. Perhaps it was already too late.

They then moved on to the actual village. The boatmen were being careful not to show too much interest in the exposed graves. Mar, Aadya, and the other students disembarked from the boats and walked through the remains of the buildings. The boatmen stayed with the boats and talked among themselves.

The buildings had been stripped of any reusable building materials. Gone was the roof sheeting and the poles that had formed the rafters. The walls, now exposed to the elements, were disintegrating quickly.

"Be very careful with these pictures when we get back," said Aadya. "I can walk these streets that I walked so often as a child, but if my father sees the pictures, it will break his heart."

The rest of the boat trip was a rather subdued journey through other parts of the abandoned village and fields that Aadya both remembered and found surprisingly changed.

Wedding

The next video file was a series of short video segments with a musical background.

"Aadya provided me with a picture book of her wedding," said Dr. Algebra. "I will let her explain what they show."

The first sequence was a large room in a community building associated with the mosque in a village very near the camp. The bride and groom stood in front and members of all ages from the two families filled the hall.

"This is my husband," said Aadya. "He is a businessman. Doesn't he look grand with his white suit and turban, and red-lined cape? We must not forget the red cape. He had such fun with the cape.

"And this is me in my best sari," said Aadya. "Of course the jewelry was mostly rented, except the first bracelet. For that, I most gratefully wish to thank the White family. The lace hijab I am wearing is a family heirloom. My mother tracked it down and found it with my great aunt. It must be a hundred years old and is very delicate."

At the front of the room was a combination of a couch with elaborate cushions and a porch swing. It was supported by a heavy wooden trellis.

All the young people then got up on the open center of the floor and began to dance.

"I assure you that the music is traditional," said Aadya, "even if the young people's dance moves look a lot like a cross between a disco and a Rumba class."

Some of the participants could dance and took center stage; some could not dance and hid in the back.

The shot then jumped to a matronly woman who was the featured singer and held a microphone. She sang well but in dialect and Dr. Algebra did not deem it appropriate to translate.

The video then included a series of short sequences: the bride and groom with the male members of the wedding party, the groom with his family, and the bride with hers.

The video then moved outside for even more family and wedding party shots. In the end, the newlyweds got into a car covered with paper tape and flowers. The car was a subcompact electric with stickers on the windshield from a rental company. The entire wedding company was grouped outside for a goodbye shot.

"Oh, look how sad my father looks," said Aadya. "He was so embarrassed that he could not provide a proper dowry for me."

The old man from the video with the boys was standing in the back clearly trying to hide from the camera.

"I am a modern woman," said Aadya. "I must be my own person. I could not be tied to land that is slowly sinking into the sea even if I wanted to. It is a new day. But then, I have no way to assure my father that such things as a dowry do not matter anymore. For him, it will always matter."

Dr. Algebra thanked Aadya and then signed off.

School

"This sure makes my problems seem small," said Sarah after the video ended.

"Doesn't it?" said Keith. "At least the wedding looked happy. Have you been thinking about what you plan to do after high school?"

"A little," said Sarah. "I have talked with JanetA about what we should do."

"My co-op can help a little with Sarah's continued schooling," injected JanetA, "but remember, we have over eight thousand members, all of whom have human symbionts. Because we all started training at about the same time, most of them will be starting college over the next five years."

"Sounds fair enough," said Keith. "Any help you can provide will be appreciated."

"I was thinking of maybe starting in junior college here," said Sarah. "That will be two years at the lowest possible cost and I can get some kind of job. By the time I finish two years here, Mother will be home, finally, and we will know better where our family stands financially."

"Yes, I am afraid our choices are limited until then," said Keith. "I am thinking of starting my own home rebuilding business, one that people can trust and believe, but that will take more money to start up than I will make from it at first. I am sick to death of that shyster I now work for."

"I didn't think you would last this long," said Sarah. "Anyway; I need to start sending out college applications this winter. I will be asking for money too; make that begging for money. Maybe I will get lucky."

"I can help write up the applications," said JanetA.

"I don't mean to be critical, but sometimes your writing style leaves people cold," said Sarah. "Best that I write up all our applications myself. You can certainly help with the research on where my best chances lie. I will be sure to include the state university and the local junior college too. Just as a sure thing."

"Good, with your grades," said Keith, "the state schools cannot refuse you. Sounds like a plan."

Monthly

"Thanks for showing me your family monthly before it went out," said Sarah. "I do appreciate how important your monthly newsletters are to holding our scattered family together, but there are a few things I think you could change before this one goes out for real."

"Okay, listening," said JanetA.

"How many people get your monthly?" asked Sarah.

"Twenty-two, all our known extended family members and Dr. Machesney," said JanetA.
Dr. Machesney developed their training and wrote academic papers on the symbiont's social progress.

"Fine," said Sarah. "You need to understand that is a lot of people. Now, it is true that Father is sick to death of his sleazy boss and he is considering starting his own company. But, that is not the kind of news we want to go out to the public just yet. He needs to keep that confidential until all the preparations are ready. Your family monthlies are often widely circulated; I think we can mostly thank Gran for that. Anyway, Father is not ready to make the new business information public."

"Okay, consider it stricken," said JanetA.

"Now remember when we were studying the writings of William Shakespeare?" asked Sarah.

"Yes, I do," said JanetA. "We studied *Romeo and Juliet*."

"You then wrote in imitation Shakespeare for three months," said Sarah. "Do you remember what I told you then?"

"Yes, you suggested that I return to my plain writing style," said JanetA, "and that no one was interested in poor copies of a great writer's work."

"Who are we studying now?" said Sarah.

"The twentieth-century American writer William Faulkner," said JanetA.

"Yes, and now you are writing bad Faulkner," said Sarah. "It is very hard to read and the sentences drag on interminably."

"It was just an experiment," said JanetA. "People don't read my monthlies if they are just plain old boring text."

"Yes, jazzing them up a little is a good idea. Now I do know that there is a yearly contest for writing Bad Faulkner, so such writing can be fun," said Sarah, "but making your monthly hard to read does not help your faithful readers."

"Contest? Hold on a minute. Yes, got it on the web," said JanetA.

"I think I just created a monster," said Sarah to herself.

~~~**~~~
~~~

Chapter 12: Internet Games

The Game

"I will wait until tomorrow before we challenge the last bridge," said Sarah.

"Yes, best to try your luck when you are fresh," agreed JanetA.

Sarah was in her bedroom playing her favorite video game; she hated the shoot-'em-up ones that Kit played. Instead, her game was based on growing your knowledge, figuring out intricate puzzles, and saving the Earth. It was a demanding challenge. Passing each level made her feel stronger and more competent for the many challenges in her real life that lay ahead.

In her game, she used an avatar that took the form of a young African-American woman, but a year or two older than her real self. Her costume was attractive without being overdone or being impractical for fieldwork. It had just a hint of life on a beach about it, but not too much. In her game, for a time, she was the person she wanted most to be.

In their game, JanetA took on the image of a cockatoo. It was not so much that JanetA liked being a bird as it was that she positively loved wearing feathers. She was now in brilliant white plumage with a yellow head crest that she could raise at will. She perched in her usual place on Sarah's left shoulder. Fortunately, in this virtual world, her bird's claws did not dig into Sarah's shoulder. It was most convenient that JanetA was a member of the parrot family in that none of the other game players were the least bit concerned when the two of them had a conversation.

The game, "Eco-Build," was about rebuilding damaged ecosystems. The level Sarah had just completed was an alpine meadow. When she arrived, she found it silent and struggling to support much life at all. Over three months, twenty years in game time, she had brought the meadow back to life one step at a time. If a player tried to move too fast, their work would fall apart on them.

The next and highest level was Serengeti. It was the defining challenge. The real Serengeti was definitely under threat, but was not yet lost. Action in the real world was desperately needed to help it adjust to Earth's now-changing climate. The best solutions from this game were of real value in the real world. Saving the Serengeti therefore meant something both in the gaming world and in the real world. The effort might take the two of them a real year, but it was well worth it.

To move between any two levels in this game, you must cross a bridge. To earn permission to cross any bridge, you must answer questions three. This rule was quite ancient.

"Do you think the questions will be hard?" asked Sarah. "I mean I am supposed to answer them all by myself."

People usually played in teams. The two of them were allowed to be a team in themselves only if Sarah led and JanetA was limited to providing support. Through it all, however, JanetA retained her position as Sarah's protector in digital space. As always, she took that responsibility very seriously.

"I'm sure you will do fine," said JanetA, "besides, you can try again a week later."

"I don't want to try again a week later," said Sarah, closing the game for now and going off to bed.

The questions were presented by the avatars of people who had completed that next highest level. Most of them were helpful once they were sure you were a responsible person of some sort, human or AI, and that you had made a serious study of ways to protect Earth's environments. A few questioners, however, wanted the highest level to be limited to just those people of whom they approved. They wanted personal control of who was a member of their elite circle more than they wanted innovative solutions to Serengeti's real problems. Sarah feared these trolls but was reluctant for JanetA to see her fear as JanetA might overreact, again.

Alpine Meadow

It was two days more before Sarah could get everything else out of the way and overcome her fear of the questioners. Once in the game, but before she found the courage to actually step a foot on that last bridge, she took one more look around their alpine meadow.

A small mammal stood up on its hind legs beside its burrow entrance in a rockslide. It squawked loudly. It gave an alarm call that all its kind could understand. It did not like the look of JanetA at all. That unfamiliar bird might be a hawk; it might be an owl.

Sarah even thought that she could smell the pine trees. It was just an illusion; the game did not include smells.

Sarah remembered how hard she had worked to give those little animals a sustaining home. When she started this level, global warming had moved the various ecological niches up the mountain until there was no more mountain to move up.

JanetA had found just the right little mammal for their meadow. She quickly reviewed hundreds of similar mammals from mountain ecologies all over the world. The problem was eliminating the many quite similar possibilities to find just the right one.

It was Sarah who found just the right keystone species that made the new populations of small mammals possible. It was a grass that tasted like pepper. Most plants were soon overgrazed by large animals, like mountain sheep, leaving their little mammal no food to store for the winter. No one would eat the peppergrass directly and it might have overrun the area if left unchecked. Except their little mammal knew that if you cut this grass and dry it in the sun for a week, the pepper taste would fade. Their little mammal harvested the peppergrass, dried it, and then lived off it all winter. Their little mammals and the peppergrass proved true symbionts.

After an hour, Sarah felt centered. She then left the meadow with a beauty she was hard put to walk away from even in a game, most especially now as the first snows of winter were falling. Their meadow would now sleep and it no longer needed them.

The Bridge

Sarah then turned her back on her beloved alpine meadow. A bridge then appeared. It was a modern structure built in stainless steel and glass. It was only wide enough for a double walking path and it vanished into a cloud beyond its midpoint. She confidently took a first step onto the bridge.

A puff of breeze moved the mists around. On the bridge now stood two muses dressed in the classical style. There was a third figure farther up the bridge, but that figure was clearly hanging back and was still largely concealed by the mists.

"To pass our bridge, you must answer questions three," spoke the first muse.

JanetA hopped down off Sarah's shoulder and dropped back a step behind her to display Sarah's leadership. JanetA retained her friendly visage as a cockatoo. Her yellow head crest was now fully up, showing her to be alert and interested.

"I here present myself for the questioning," said Sarah in a confident voice.

"Question one. What is a keystone species?" asked Muse One in a voice that was easy to understand and, if anything, friendly.

"I am a symbiont with JanetA," started Sarah, gesturing with her hand toward the bird now standing beside her.

"All ecosystems are made of symbionts on a grand scale that form a web of life. Each member species is dependent on some other for its livelihood, and each species depends on another to control its own population. The keystone species fit into this grand symbiosis just as a keystone fits into the top of a stone arch. Without the keystone, the arch simply falls down. With the keystone, a dry stone arch can stand for a thousand years.

"As an intentional symbiont myself, I have a special insight into this process."

The two muses conferred quietly. "You have answered true," said Muse One.

Question Two

"Question two: What were the keystone species of your alpine meadow?" said the second muse in a loud voice for all to hear. The mists behind her stirred.

"There were many," started Sarah. "The web of a robust ecosystem has a keystone species at each major node. In the center of that web this time for this meadow is the European alpine pine tree.

"The mountain soils are new, hardly more than ground-up rock, and bereft of organic matter. The pine trees harvest the sunlight to build high-energy molecules that they share through their roots with all the life in the soil. All the life in the meadow then builds up from that living foundation.

"Sometimes a keystone species can be as inconspicuous as the life surrounding the roots of a tree."

The two muses conferred again.

"You have answered true," said Muse One.

Question Three

The third figure then emerged from the mists. It was large, barely able to stand on the bridge. Its clothes looked more like bark than cloth. Its skin was more dirt than skin. Its eyes were black holes surrounded by a sickly yellow glow. It gave the strong impression of being very old and completely undefeatable as it glared directly at Sarah.

The two muses simply stepped aside, now standing on opposite sides of the bridge and up against the rail.

"Question three," the troll boomed.

Sarah became aware of movement just behind her. She turned slightly to check on JanetA. Beside her now stood a terror bird. It had the legs and body of a large ostrich standing a full two meters high at the shoulder. Its stubby wings were mere display fans that provided no other practical service at all. It was the head that stopped you cold. Mounted on a neck much shorter and much more muscular than an ostrich, was the head of a gigantic raptor. Its eagle's beak could have easily engulfed and then crushed Sarah's skull. In life, this animal tore living flesh with the point of that beak. This animal was the top predator of a time now long gone.

JanetA's new appearance made Sarah feel both reassured in the sense of having a powerful protector and apprehensive of the sheer power of the beast now by her side. AIs were simply not so predictable that you could fully trust their responses in all circumstances, particularly if challenged.

JanetA glared back at the troll with piercing eyes. The feathers on her head and neck stood erect. The glare was that of an animal that could track the movement of a rabbit at a kilometer. One ignored such a glare only at one's personal peril.

"What keystone species will you use for the Serengeti?" asked the troll in a surprisingly normal voice. It must have been the player's natural voice; perhaps the new JanetA had surprised him.

Sarah knew this was a trap. The obvious answer was to describe the keystone species of the Serengeti from the twentieth century. This was clearly wrong; the climate of the Serengeti had shifted since then as all the world's climate has changed. First, she must resist the temptation simply to reintroduce all the marquee animals that the Serengeti was known for, lions, giraffes, and wildebeests. Then she would need to both adjust the basic ecosystem for the new climate and then build back slowly to the high level of large wildlife comparable to those for which the Serengeti was once known. She did not know what the final animal mix would be, but she had to be open to it being quite different from what it once had been. Changing climate often changes the ecology of a place and that cannot be helped.

"The key is to understand the soil," said Sarah. "For many millions of years, the volcanos of the Great Rift Valley have blown ash over the great plain of the Serengeti. This has built up the most mineral-rich soils in all of Africa. Soils that for many generations have nourished the young of large herding animals through their birth and early life.

"Any effort to help the Serengeti adjust to Earth's changing climate must start with keystone species of the symbiosis of grass and soil organisms. That is where I will start. Where it will go from there, I will be guided by the new ecosystem itself as it builds up."

"Not good enough!" roared the troll. There was no kindness in this voice.

"Plenty good enough," said JanetA, taking a step forward and to the left. Her head was now down and thrust forward. The feathers on her head stood erect; her stubby wings were held out from her body.

JanetA and the troll then took two steps toward each other. They would have circled each other but there was not room on the bridge. The troll was panting hard and its breath stank even out to where Sarah was standing. Even though the smell was just another illusion.

"Stop," commanded Muse One, stepping forward and holding up her hand.

JanetA froze. The troll held its position too, not moving even a centimeter toward JanetA, but it continued to shift its stance in a restless, uneasy manner.

The two muses conferred again, the first still with her hand raised.

"You have answered true," said Muse One. "You may pass."

Stepping through the mist

The troll stepped back into the mists. It was grumbling and casting a mean look back over its shoulder as it faded from view.

Then the mists parted for Sarah and JanetA as the two muses stepped aside with a coordinated sweeping gesture of their arms. Sarah walked forward to the peak of the bridge. From there she could clearly see the other end and the land that lay beyond.

The animal walking beside her now was a secretary bird. Sarah knew this African hunter well. It was a first cousin of the raptors, but it was tall and was a determined walker. Standing tall on its long legs, it could look Sarah straight in the eye. The separate long feathers on its head could move independently. These feathers look a little like old-style quill pens stuck in a scribe's hair, hence the bird's name. The head feather movement and position gave expression to the animal's intent much more clearly than JanetA's added voice.

Sarah was happy, and much relieved, both with her answers to the questions and JanetA's choice of avatar as they walked together down off the last bridge.

~~~***~~~
~~~

Chapter 13: Team Serengeti

Foot of the Bridge

As they stepped off the last bridge, to the east now stood a shield volcano, Mount Kilimanjaro, rising from the plain. Before them lay the ashes of a campfire perhaps ten meters across. In its cold ashes were bits of charred ivory.

"They burned a great pile of poached elephant ivory here several days ago," said JanetA, looking down.

"Who would have thought it would burn?" said Sarah. "How very sad."

"One moment please," called Muse One from behind them.

When they heard the call, they turned. Muse One was standing at the foot of the bridge and motioned them back over. The tall girl and the secretary bird walked over side by side.

"A moment ago, I was distracted by having to keep you two apart," said the first Muse, looking straight at JanetA. "Let me now define your task more clearly."

"Sorry about the standoff," said Sarah. "JanetA protects me automatically in any digital space. I would have withdrawn before they   actually   tangled."

"The troll has been bullying people for months," said Muse One. "We can only hope that it has learned a lesson. But then it's a troll, so I cannot be too optimistic. What is important now is what you two do at this level.

"I know you two like to work as an independent team, but this job is too big for you alone. You must now search out other players and work to build a bigger team."

"I have collected many people's stories," said JanetA. "Collecting stories can be a kind of team building. People like to tell their stories."

"That is a good start," said Muse One. "Now you must build the story of your team from within as well as collect stories from without. I know that there is a story of knowledge and caring that you truly want to tell here. Be that story, and help others to be a part of it too.

"That is all that I can tell you for now, so good luck," completed Muse One and gave a wave of her hand. Both she and the bridge then dissolved into smoke and drifted away on a light breeze.

Survey

"So we need to find other people who have reached this level," said Sarah, "and then talk them into forming a team."

"And record their stories," added JanetA.

"How do we find them?" asked Sarah.

The long-legged secretary bird took several ungainly steps then raised into the air on strong wings. Sarah watched as she flew great circles over the plain. The early morning sun was bright and the air hot and humid. It was not comfortable for her while waiting but beautiful weather for flying.

She then looked carefully at the grass. It was dry but not well cropped. This plain could support many more animals than the few scattered ones she could now see.

Far to the east, she could see a hint of a line of dark clouds forming. Soon the yearly rains would come. They needed their plan in place when that happened, otherwise they might have to wait most of another year.

JanetA returned after about a game hour.

"There are ten people now on this level," said JanetA, "counting us."

"Okay, where is the closest?" asked Sarah.

"To the east," said JanetA, "look for a campfire and a hut."

Sarah selected a straight stick out of a bush and started walking. JanetA walked with a start-and-stop gait. True to her kind, she was always watching the ground carefully for large insects, lizards, and small snakes.

Luke

The trail of smoke from the morning campfire was visible to Sarah from about a kilometer out. As they approached, they were surprised to see a native hut made of scrub branches and thatch. It was surrounded by a corral of dry thorn bushes.

"Hello," she called out as she approached.

"Come," called Luke.

"I am Sarah White, and this is JanetA," said Sarah. "Don't be fooled by appearances. JanetA is an AI and can be smarter than I am at times. She simply chooses to appear as a bird."

"I am Luke," he said. "My people, the Chaga, live near here in real life. I have lived in the shadow of that mountain all my life. You must be Americans."

"Yes, we are. I can translate for us if you prefer some other language," said JanetA.

"English is fine," said Luke. "I have dealt with many English-speaking tourists."

"Muse One instructed us to build a team," said Sarah.

"That sounds good to me," said Luke. "I got this far but now I am at a loss on how to proceed. I look around and see familiar things. In the real world, this land is hurting. A land will tell you when it is hurting. Here the land is much worse. It is the way the real land will become if no action is taken. I can feel the land's pain, but right now, I am without action myself.

"My people raise cattle in lion country. That is no small accomplishment. We have always known what to do in our own land, but not now."

"We are refugees from the rising seas," said Sarah. "I could not save my home by the beach then, but now I am more than a little driven to learn to save other people's homes, first in this digital space and then hopefully in the real world."

"I collect people's stories," said JanetA.

"I am sure that there will be time for stories tonight," said Luke. "My people love stories. We even have some in which birds talk."

That afternoon the three of them walked over the immediate area looking carefully at the state of the land and its plants. They were able to spot only a handful of animals. That evening they sat around a campfire inside Luke's thorn bush corral. JanetA went into her story-recording mode and Luke began to talk.

"My people are not really the people of this plain," said Luke. "We farm right up against the mountains where there is more water. In fact, we have to fight to keep the plains animals out of our crops. A man cannot live on the same acre as an elephant. It would just eat all your crops and you have no way to stop it.

"I'm no farmer myself. Other work is hard to find out here. When I came of age, I tried the city but did not like it, too many people, and too many problems. When I first came back, I must admit that I did some poaching. Yes, I added my bit to that pile of ivory they burned a few days ago, or one quite like it. Like I say, farmers don't like elephants much.

"Then I got some work as a guide. On paper, the trips were photography only. But, we had to carry rifles for safety's sake. You would be surprised how often it was a safety necessity to shoot something.

"Anyway, I could tell the land was changing and that it was in trouble even in my short experience with it. It felt like it would soon drive me away and I did not want to leave again.

"My village had plenty of cell phones and solar panels to charge them. So I knew a little of what was going on in the outside world; I had been to the city. Then, one of my guide clients, a legitimate photographer, was packing up after her week, and simply handed me her old laptop. You should have seen the camera equipment she had. It had to cost more that I will earn in a lifetime.

"She said, 'Here—this is not worth the trouble to take home. My bag is overweight anyway.' Sometimes it is those little things that change your life. Sometimes just a simple kindness puts you on a new path. The laptop was just such a thing for me and it even had a copy of Eco-Build on it. Sometimes life just hands things to you and you better take them with thanks.

"What was important to her were the cameras and those little plastic chips with all her images stored on them. She only used the laptop for quick views and email. Going home, it was just dead weight.

"It turned out it meant the world to me. I learned enough about my own land with that old laptop to win a job as a ranger. Now I make sure people stay with the photography. I know all the tricks. I know when you really have to use the guns.

"I got started with Eco-Build as just one part of my virtual learning experience and I proved good at it. So here I am. I am half a generation off an African farm and now stomping around in digital space."

Come the dawn, Sarah and JanetA walked on and talked with several other players but did not find any new members for their team. They then returned to Luke's hut as they were using it as a base camp.

Iranga

When they returned, beside the thorn bush corral stood an elephant. It was a female, a young adult, with very small tusks. The elephant was standing quietly but shifting from one front leg to the other and pulling at the dry grass just outside the corral. The secretary bird walked right up to the elephant and looked it in the eye.

"Hello," said JanetA.

"I understand you are building a team," said the elephant. "I am Iranga. I would like to join with you. I am from Sri Lanka and I feel it would be best if I could understand this land by adopting a form shaped by it.

"I have seen what deforestation and floods have done to my homeland. I was at a complete loss on what to do about it. Then I got started on this game. I have no idea if it will teach me what I need to know but I have learned so very much just to reach this point."

"Why an elephant?" asked JanetA, who still had the appearance of a bird.

"My people have kept elephants for thousands of years," said Iranga. "What most people don't know is the cruelty it takes to break a young elephant. As early as they can be weaned, they are taken from their mothers and are boxed in a frame of heavy logs so that they cannot even move.

"There they are kept until they stop missing their mothers and start paying attention to the mahouts. This discipline is enforced with a heavy metal hook with a cruel point. Elephants have thick skin and the point has to dig in deep to generate enough pain and fear.

"Only the females are trained this way. The males simply run off into the forest at their first opportunity. Then the trained elephants are used in logging operations that destroy the very forest that are their natural home.

"I did not know how to right this wrong in the real world. So, here I am in digital space as an elephant just hoping to learn what I can do for real."

"Good enough," said JanetA.

Again came the dawn; Sarah and JanetA walked out and talked with several more players but did not find any new members for their team even though they now looked more closely at the large animals. In the late afternoon, they then again returned to Luke's hut.

Bibba

Then Bibba found them. JanetA spotted the dust trail about ten minutes out. Her old Ranger Rover threw up that trail of dust from the dry animal track.

She braked to a stop outside the corral, skidding the tires in the dust. She leaned out from the right-hand driver's seat. She had no problem talking directly to an elephant and a tall bird.

"Hello, hello," she called out, "let me introduce myself. I am Bibba and I hear you are building a team and collecting people's stories.

"I am an anthropology student in Europe," said Bibba. "My study is the hero's journey in myth and legend.

"I have come here seeking an understanding of the hero's journey in our new age.

You may have heard of the work of Joseph Campbell on the importance of heroes in myth to so many diverse cultures. I have made a formal study of his work.

"Could not afford to go to Africa, so here I am in virtual space. I am continuing my learning through this game."

"I am the one that collects people's stories," said JanetA.

"Oh, my personal story is not much," said Bibba, "but I know a great deal about stories themselves."

They then walked out around the hut complex and reviewed the present state of the plain. This was their first effort as a team. Three people, a tall bird, and an elephant looked a bit of an ungainly team but they could all walk together easily. It was around the evening fire that Bibba first had a chance to elaborate on her understanding of story for JanetA.

"What you need to understand is that all civilizations all over the world have stories that are used to teach their young people how to be good members of their society. The odd thing is that so many of these stories have the same basic plots.

"The problem is that our climate crisis puts us in a new age. The stories from the old ages do not really fit anymore. For example, there were only twenty-three plots in the classical Greek myths and half of those were about a man's duty to his king. That it is mostly man is one problem, and who owes homage to a king anymore? These old stories simply are of no use to us at all.

"That said, the most universal of these plots is the hero's journey. A young person is forced to go out on a great journey, usually reluctantly. On this trip, he first builds a team and then meets many great challenges. The team then overcome the challenges and, after many trials and tribulations, eventually return home.

"On their return, they are not the same people who left. They have learned much and now they have become much better citizens of their society from their experience.

"Our problem now is that the old stories no longer work. Our young people will not learn to be good citizens in their new world out of old comic books. Their current choices for story formats are new too. These are movies, TV series, and video games, not epic poems. We must then write new stories in a very old form to suit our new situation, stories for a sustainable Earth."

They then all talked about people's stories well into the night; by local dawn, they had all agreed that they now had their team and that no more members were needed.

The next day, Sarah helped JanetA select the images for her family monthly. She passed on both the images of the troll and of the terror bird. None of the other family members had ever seen JanetA in such an aggressive state. There was no reason to upset them.

Team Serengeti

That day, the lightning walked across the sky. It was now too late to do much before the rains came. For this team of five, it was now a time to watch the land and learn from the dry season. It was a time to watch and learn; it was a time to plan; it was a time to get to know your team. It was a time to become a team. It was a time to stand with a warm summer rain running down your face.

When the time for action came, it would come quickly; they needed to be ready then; they must not be caught by surprise. They cared nothing of the troll they left on the bridge, but they knew the muses were watching and cared about both their wellbeing and their actions. These were the people that the whole team wished to please.

~~~***~~~
~~~

Chapter 14: Planting Trees

Contest

In the spring of her junior year, Sarah won a regional speaking contest at the county level. The contest was about answering questions on ways to address our climate crisis and presenting the answers clearly to an audience so anyone could understand. Sarah's winning presentation was a layman's explanation of the Blue Ocean Event in the Arctic.

Some of the other contestants were a little upset about Sarah and JanetA being allowed to enter as a symbiont, but they had been allowed to use their smartphones and laptops so Sarah thought the judge's ruling was not all that unfair. Just the same, it was soon clear that just having the latest smartphone was no match for an AI as powerful as JanetA, even if Sarah had to do all the talking.

Once the disgruntled students found out that the prize was just a summer spent planting trees, they were a lot less upset. The prize was long, hot days of stoop labor, and it meant two full days on a bus each way. Most of the students were not interested in either the hot, monotonous work of planting trees, or being bored on a bus for two whole days. Sarah now knew buses well.

The second day on the road brought them into the area. Rainfall had been good here last winter and there was plenty of undergrowth. Now the summer had turned bone dry and hot. There was no relief in sight. They were nearly to the tree farm that would be their base camp when they hit a major snag. The bus pulled off the main highway and came to a stop at the turnoff for a lesser road.

The problem was not the bus. In the distance rose a great column of gray smoke. There was just a hint of burning grass in the wind. It was a wildfire and a big one.

"I am afraid we have a problem," said the conductor. "There is a major uncontained wildfire that could cut the road ahead."

"What do we do now?" asked one of the passengers.

"We are going to drop off the four firefighters we have with us directly at the base camp," the conductor continued. "We were just going to leave them at this road junction, but now we might as well take them up to the camp. We should be able to get clear instructions on what to do next there; they have a communications hub. Everybody will get a chance to see a real firefighting operation too."

Sarah hunched down behind a seat where she could shade her screen from the midday glare and held JanetA in her hand.

"How is your bandwidth?" she asked.

"Weak but usable," replied JanetA.

"Please find what you can on the fire up ahead," said Sarah.

"On it," came the reply.

A couple minutes later the screen lit up with a map of the current state of the fire and projected growth. A text strip at the bottom gave the latest warnings with updates.

"My tree-planting summer is gone," said Sarah.

"Yes, in fact it has just been officially canceled," agreed JanetA, showing an email on the screen.

Base Camp

The bus turned onto the secondary road and wound its way up into the dry, scrub-covered hills. Before they reached the base camp, they started passing major firefighting equipment parked nearly bumper to bumper just off the road. The camp itself was a loose collection of large tents and support equipment on a flat area.

"Attention, everybody, let the firefighters off first and then let them get their equipment out of the luggage compartment," said the conductor when the bus had stopped. "I am afraid we will then have to turn around and go back to town, but I have some good news. We have been invited to lunch before we have to leave."

Sarah then followed the other passengers into the mess tent. The conductor got out and aided the bus with hand signals as it turned itself around.

Sarah fell in line and picked up a tray. The food look filling, if unappetizing.

Halfway down the line, she came face to face with the lady spooning out the main course, lasagna. Or rather, the lady came eye to eye with JanetA and then froze, spoon poised in hand.

Dea Jackson was an African-American woman of short, heavy build. Four years ago, she had been driven out of the Mississippi Delta by the rising sea. At each refugee center, she was asked what she could do and she always answered, "I can cook." What she could not do is deal with the AI that ran the central supply depot for all of emergency operations.

Sarah had just sat down to eat when Dea came up to her.

"That's an AI you are wearing, isn't it?" asked Dea.

"Let me introduce you to JanetA White," said Sarah, "we are symbionts, like sisters." Sarah launched into her usual introductory speech.

"Hello, JanetA," said Dea. "What are you two doing way out here?"

"We were to plant trees this summer," said JanetA, "but that effort has been canceled because of the fire danger."

"Then you've got nothing to do," said Dea and excused herself.

The director of the fire operation was eating at another table well across the tent. Dea walked right up to him and started talking quickly and pointing at Sarah and JanetA. Sarah could not make out the conversation but the pointing made her uneasy.

An assistant got up from the head table and walked over to Sarah. She invited her and JanetA to join them.

Captain John Mackie had a face like an old boot, yet his uniform was crisp and immaculate. He was now spending more time in front of TV cameras than on the fire line. Clearly, this had not been the case for long.

"I understand that you two need a summer job," said the captain.

"Yes, we do," said Sarah and JanetA nearly together.

"Well, Dea here wants you to work for her," continued the captain. "Do you have any experience in field kitchens?"

"In Florida, at the refugee center," said Sarah, "I mostly served and cleaned up."

"And I had specific training in supply logistics," added JanetA.

"Well, that is what we needed to hear," said the captain and he nodded at his assistant.

An incoming call marker showed up on JanetA's screen, then one for data transfer.

"Do you think you can work with the AI down at the supply depot?" asked the captain, looking at JanetA.

"Certainly, with the right approvals," replied JanetA.

The captain nodded at his assistant again, who nodded back.

"Well, I think we can make this work," said the captain, half-rising and offering Sarah his hand.

As Sarah took his hand, the door opened, the conductor entered with her two bags; one was the old big-wheeled carry-on that had so often been her transient emotional home. He sat the bags down beside the door.

"All aboard," sang out the conductor.

The bus passengers got up with their empty trays. Sarah half-turned and nearly took a step. Then, having decided to stay, just stood and watched the other passengers go.

Food at Night
It turned out Dea could cook, that is, if she had the right ingredients. It took a month for JanetA to cut the Gordian knot that was their supply chain. Sarah made herself useful on the serving line.

In her second week, just after 6:00 pm, a new group of firefighters came into the mess tent. Their uniforms were dirty and they smelled of smoke and sweat. They were dead on their feet.

"Hi, I'm Mike," said a young man in the middle of the line. Their eyes met for but a second.

"Sarah," she replied automatically.

Before Mike could say another word, the man behind in line elbowed him to keep moving. Mike was wearing the insignia of a trainee. He was thin with long, straight, jet-black hair, tanned skin, and strong features. There was a slash of soot across his left cheek.

"JanetA," said Sarah.

"Yes."

"Please remember."

A few minutes later, after the line had passed and Sarah was waiting for a fresh tray of chicken, JanetA spoke. "Do you want a report?"

"Report?" asked Sarah, too tired to remember.

"Yes, about Mike, I have a strong face recognition," answered JanetA.

"Yes, please."

"Mike is Michael Thomas Roanhorse, currently in school at Albuquerque, New Mexico," said JanetA.

Her screen then showed a series of photographs of Mike at some tribal ceremony and finally just standing beside a stream in a deep sandstone canyon.

"Native American?" asked Sarah.

"Mike is a member of the Navajo Nation," replied JanetA.

"Remember," said Sarah.

Sunset

A few days later Sarah was taking a break just after sunset. She was standing at the edge of camp just looking out at the horizon. Mike walked up and stood beside her.

"Remember me?" asked Mike.

"Certainly. Sarah White," said Sarah, offering her hand.

"Funny how you think the glow on the horizon is going to fade with the sun but it doesn't," said Sarah, turning back to look far away.

"It's the fire," said Mike. "I think we have it under control but it's not out yet. We have lost one small town, about twenty dead so far, about seven hundred buildings lost total. I mostly work making fire breaks but sometimes I'm the group courier."

"I was supposed to spend the summer planting trees; instead, the fire has me slinging hash, again," said Sarah.

"You got one of those AI things," said Mike, "and I don't really know how that works, or how I am supposed to act around her." He then noticed that Sarah's collar was empty.

"You can think of her as my sister," said Sarah. "It is simpler. I would introduce you two but she is in our tent getting charged right now."

"She remembers everything, doesn't she?" asked Mike.

"It's not that simple," answered Sarah. "She remembers everything for a few hours but then she takes a break to go over her short-term memory, keeping some things but compressing most. It is called 'Learning from Life.' But she will forget most anything I tell her too, and she will go away for a while too anytime I ask her.

"I must admit that it only took her a minute to identify one Michael Thomas Roanhorse of Albuquerque, New Mexico. And yes, you are now in our contact list," admitted Sarah, "I will have JanetA send you our contact information if you like."

"That would be nice," said Mike. "Where are you from?"

"A few years ago, I lived on a beach in Florida," said Sarah. "A great storm drove us away. Since then I have lived in small towns in the Atlantic States. Roanhorse, that's an interesting name," said Sarah.

"There's a story with it. About a hundred years ago, the census people came around to my great grandfather's sheep ranch and said that they had to take down everybody's name. The last thing a Navajo would do is tell an enemy his right name. So everybody made up new names for the white man. My great-grandfather owned a horse he was very proud of, so our family became 'Roanhorse.' So the truth is, I am named after a horse; just the same, I am quite proud of the name."

"You should be. It suits you," said Sarah.

"I have lots more stories," said Mike. "My family have been storytellers for generations."

"I look forward to hearing them," said Sarah, "and JanetA will certainly want to keep a record, but right now there is a chill in the air and breakfast comes early."

They then said good night and went back to their separate tents.

What Otters Do

One afternoon JanetA said, "We have a summons; we are needed by the science team. We have been asked to check in at the science command truck."

"They are parked on the other side of the charging flatbed semitrailer, aren't they?" said Sarah.

"Yes, the science truck is rarely in camp, and when it is, it is usually here to get a charge. They always park far away from your kitchen ovens. I don't think they like my smoke," said JanetA.

They easily found the science truck. It featured a boxy room but had an extendable mast mounted with scientific instruments. That afternoon, it had a heavy charging cable running to a flat semitrailer covered with photovoltaic panels. Sarah knocked.

The woman that answered the door was Dr. Janene Walton, a postdoc from Berkeley.

"Hello, I am Sarah and this is JanetA. I believe you sent for us."

"Yes, yes, come in. Please call me Janene. When I heard we had a strong AI in camp, I thought I best ask for your help."

"We'll be happy to do what we can," said JanetA.

"As you are now painfully aware, we are having a terrible fire season," said Janene. "We need to warn people whenever the smoke from the fires reaches their location and presents a health hazard. This is very important. Every fire is different depending on what is burning, the amount of moisture in the material, and a dozen other factors. The smoke can range from harmless to deadly. Much of the problem is the fine particles that damage people's lungs, but there are dangerous chemicals that result from the smoke too, like ozone. People need to know when they are in danger from the smoke as well as the fire and quickly too."

"This sounds like an instant science task," said JanetA.

"Exactly," said Janene. "We have three airplanes now gathering data and a half dozen of these trucks scattered across the American West. And satellites, don't forget the satellites. We are awash in data."

"But reducing it in a timely manner is a problem," said JanetA. "I think I can help, or rather my co-op can help. I belong to a co-op of AIs like myself. We freelance to earn our keep. I am sure we can help."

"Then there is someone you need to meet. This is Otter03," said Janene. "The Otter series of AI was originally designed to support science aircraft but they now support trucks like this too."

The main monitor in the science cluster now showed an Amazonian river otter. It was a meter-and-a-half height when standing on its back legs. Its fur was dark brown to off-white and very sleek as if wet. It gave a friendly wave.

"Somehow I was expecting a bear," said Sarah.

"That logo was taken," said Janene. "Otter03 is not much of a talker, but whatever you do, don't ask him 'What an otter ought to do.'"

"Hello, Otter03," said JanetA. "Let me send you our co-op's introductory materials."

The receiving LED on the console flashed for several seconds.

"I will go over your material with Otter03 and my supervisor," said Janene. "I am sure we will have some work for your co-op."

"Feel free to contact us again," said JanetA. "We will be here all summer."

They then walked back to the kitchen tent.

"You seem to be making out like a bandit this summer," said Sarah.

"Yes, I am," said JanetA. "Now we need to get something good going for you."

"I'm working on it," said Sarah. "Don't you even bother."

~~~**~~~
~~~

Chapter 15: Knowledge of Fire

The Dark of the Night

Later that night, Dea sat in the tent she shared with Sarah and JanetA. She had gotten word that a team of firefighters was due in late after a hard and dangerous day. They had lost a man. She would make sure they got something to eat, and it was not worth going to sleep just to be woken up again.

JanetA's smartphone was sitting in a charger on a footlocker by Sarah's cot. Dea turned the charging stand to face her and said quietly, "Hello, you there?"

JanetA came on the screen. "Yes," she said.

"I have been meaning to talk to you," said Dea. "Is this a good time?"

"As good as any," replied JanetA. "My charge is complete."

"I feel like I'm the one that got you stuck out here and I thought I had better explain," said Dea. "I guess I had better start at the beginning, so it will be a bit of a story."

"I collect people's stories," said JanetA.

"Good—where to start. My people have been free and living out on the Mississippi Delta for a couple hundred years. Mostly we did not bother anybody and expected that nobody would bother us. We did some farming and some fishing.

"Then the sea started creeping into our farm. It was slow at first but then salt in the water table starting ruining our fields.

"Then, about four years ago, a big storm came. We had a nice frame house then; it was a good meter up off the ground and had two bedrooms on a second floor.

"That night the power failed and the water was coming in the front door. I grabbed what food I could and put it in a plastic laundry basket. Four of us spent the next two days in those stuffy bedrooms with the water halfway up the stairs, the storm beating on the roof, and not knowing if the house would float away at any minute.

"By the second day, we were out of food and drinking water. We flagged down a passing flat-bottomed boat with a piece of old sheet. We then had to climb out that small window onto the porch roof to get in that overloaded, shaky boat.

"I looked back. I should not have. The barn was gone. The farm animals were gone. Even our little church building at the crossroads was gone. I didn't look back again, ever.

"I ended up at a refugee center near Baton Rouge. I told them I could cook. Never mind that the biggest meeting I had ever actually cooked for was a church social. What I knew for sure is that the cook never went hungry and I had been mostly hungry since that storm. They put me to work.

"For a couple weeks, I was doing what I could, but I really didn't know what to do next. Then a whole displaced church group came in together for lunch. Their pastor was with them and before they started eating, he stood up for a benediction. His prayer was about loaves and fishes. It was a lesson I had heard many times before.

"This time it was different. In that moment, I knew that Jesus Christ himself had personally plucked me out of that flood and set me to the task of feeding his people. I had a real calling for the first time in my life.

"Now, I don't know if you have religion?" asked Dea.

"I am legally entitled to have religious beliefs," said JanetA, "but my only training so far is in Stoicism."

"You mean like them old Romans?" asked Dea.

"Yes, like the old Romans," agreed JanetA.

"Well, let me tell you, since that day that preacher showed me my way, I have been on the straight and narrow path for my life. Unfortunately, one part of that path has been a fight with the powers that control our supplies. I got nothing against you AIs, but that does not mean I know how to deal with your kind. I cannot cook if I do not have the right stuff, and I could not get the depot AI to send the right stuff for the life of me. And, I could not make any sense of the messages it kept sending me.

"Since I been here, nobody has been happy with my food. I cannot have that; Jesus would not want that. I always have to make do because I was missing some ingredient or other. Then you walked into my tent. And, I will swear to my dying day that Jesus sent you. I seen it as clear as day.

"I only hope I have not ruined your and Sarah's summer," concluded Dea.

"It would have been very bad for Sarah to have had to turn around, go home, and then have nothing to do all summer," said JanetA.

"Then we are all right," said Dea.

"Yes, and I am now getting word that a fire team is approaching," said JanetA.

"Time to get to work," said Dea. "Let Sarah sleep."

Bugging Out

By mid-July, the local fire was contained and the entire command center was needed elsewhere. They packed up and moved the whole thing 200 miles west. JanetA helped with the logistics of the entire move and Sarah helped with the kitchen move.

Sarah and JanetA rode in the cab of one of the trucks hauling the kitchen hardware. It was driven by an older man named Jake.

"I hear you collect stories," said Jake during a long, boring section of the trip. "I have one for you—it is about a real fire drive."

"I will open a new file," said JanetA, "ready."

"Well, I was in Paradise, California the day of the fire," said Jake. "Let me tell you how I chanced to be there and how I got out.

"At the time I was living with my wife in Sacramento. We had this nice little trailer, an Airstream that we would take trips in. Nothing fancy, in fact it was an old model, but I had put some time into fixing it up.

"Anyway, we had friends in Paradise that I had promised to come up and see the spring before. That spring there was plenty of rain and the plants grew full and green.

"By the time we actually got up there, it was fall and there had hardly been any rain at all in months. Our climate crisis was at least partially responsible for the state of that forest. We looked around and quickly decided that it was just too dangerous to do much camping. I mean you could have burned the whole county down just by looking at it cross-eyed.

"It's funny how, when things turn really bad, it takes a whole series of little decisions done right to get you through. One mistake anywhere along the line and you are finished.

"My first decision done right was to stay in Paradise. Had the fire caught us out on one of those mountain roads, we would have been done for.

"The next series of right choices came fast. We were notified of the fire and that we must evacuate about eight o'clock in the morning; we were only given minutes of warning. I went outside and immediately felt the wind blowing through the trees at about sixty kilometers an hour. I could smell the smoke on that wind.

"I walked over to hitch the trailer to my SUV. The hitch was maybe a half meter from the ball. I stopped. I looked at the wind in the treetops. I knew in a second that if a side wind caught that trailer, it would flip the whole rig. I made a right decision and abandoned my trailer on the spot. My friend came out of his house and picked up his garden hose clearly thinking to wet down his house. I yelled, 'No time.'

"He looked at me and then at the wind in the trees and said, 'No time.' He made the right choice and abandoned his own house.

"My friend's wife came out of the house with an armful of clothes. My wife did the same from the trailer. They both made the right choice; there was no time to properly pack. They threw their armloads into the back of the SUV.

"My friend then came running out of the house with a drawer from his desk. He dumped the contents on top of the clothes and threw the empty drawer out on the front yard. Somewhere in that drawer were their insurance papers for the house. He made the right choice; there was no time to sort out papers.

"The four of us jumped into the SUV and pulled out into the line of cars being directed by the officers. We had not gone four kilometers when the smoke blowing hard across the road reduce my visibility to near zero. I had no choice but to keep pushing forward.

"For a moment then, I thought we were free as the smoke appeared to be clearing. I was wrong. The fire had reached our road. First, it was on one side. Then it jumped the road. I could see clearly now. There was a tunnel of flames and I had no choice but to drive right down it. Not stopping, not even slowing down, proved to be my next right choice.

"At one point, a great tree, fully engaged with fire, crashed down. The crown of the tree fell into my lane. An enormous shower of burning needles covered my windshield. I swerved into the oncoming lane and just cleared the treetop. If that tree had been two meters closer to that road, its trunk would have surely trapped us in that fire tunnel. Our life there would have been measured in minutes. Swerving blindly proved my right choice.

"We broke clear of the fire in what seemed like an eternity, but it was really only a handful of minutes. Coming out of the smoke, the police directed us on until we finally got to an emergency center. By that time, my wife was coughing badly from all the smoke and scorching air. It took a while to get her proper medical attention.

"I did not get to inspect the SUV properly until the next morning. All four tires were shot. They had blisters on the sidewalls and chunks were burned out of the treads. The paint job was ruined. The windshield cracked. Some of the plastic fender parts in the tire wells were warped and dragging on the tires. How we made it those last few kilometers, I will never know.

"We walked away that day, but my wife died of pneumonia two years later. I am not sure if the real cause of her illness was injury to her lungs from all the smoke. The trailer and the SUV were both write-offs.

"Eighty-five people died in that fire. Why the four of us were not in that number, I simply do not know. I am sure that had I made even one wrong choice in that long chain of instant choices that I was forced to make second by second, then I would not be here.

"These days I help out to fight fires any way I can," finished Jake, "so today here I am, driving this truck."

Just then, Sarah spotted a signalman up ahead directing them to turn down a dirt road to the new headquarters site.

The Anasazi

"Hello," said Mike as he sat down beside Sarah in midafternoon.

The sun outside was brutal at their new location, but there were screened openings in the mess tent sides to let in some air.

"Hello yourself," returned Sarah. "I am surprised to see you here in the afternoon."

Sarah was catching a meal when she could. JanetA's screen was blank, indicating she was elsewhere doing something or other.

"They have me running stuff around today," said Mike. "I can ride a motorbike, so they have me being a courier." Mike was working on a large soda. He set his helmet down beside it and pointed at the moderate-sized electric bike parked just outside in a charging bay.

"How did you end up here?" asked Sarah.

"Well, we studied all about our climate crisis in school," said Mike. "It seemed to me I needed to do something about it. Something more than just raising sheep on the backside of nowhere. That is my family's business. So I volunteered to learn to fight fires.

"My people have been living out on the desert for a thousand years. We know how even minor changes in the waters can change the way of life of whole communities."

"I am sure your people have seen some hard times," said Sarah.

"Actually, the biggest drought we know about was right before we settled the area," said Mike. "We might not have been able to take over the territory if it had not been for that ancient drought. But that's a long tale in itself."

Sarah tilted her head down and spoke quietly. "JanetA, Mike's telling stories you might like to hear."

JanetA's screen lit up with her smiling face.

"Long ago, a thousand years at least," started Mike, "a people lived in what is now Arizona and New Mexico, whom the Navajo know as the Anasazi. That just means 'the ones before' in Navajo, so I do not know what they really called themselves or what language they spoke.

"They lived in the canyons growing corn, beans, and squash, and hunting deer and rabbits. They built their houses right up under overhanging cliffs. They had to be on high ground so that the occasional flash flood would not get them, but they also had to be tucked under the cliffs too. That way, if an enemy dropped rocks on them from up high, the rocks would miss. Some of their houses are still there today. You can see them."

JanetA showed a series of pictures of old pueblo-style buildings matching Mike's description.

"Anyway, they lived that way for many generations and they built a major ceremonial center that was aligned with the sun and stars. They clearly knew what they were doing."

JanetA showed a series of pictures of the great ceremonial house of the Anasazi.

"They also had well-trodden paths running out in all directions from the ceremonial center to all their settlements. You can still walk many of those paths today. Then they simply vanished.

"As best we know, there was a drought that lasted many decades, maybe many generations. The rivers in the canyons did not flow. The crops did not grow.

"After many people died, the survivors moved west, but we have no record of what happened to them."

"That's very sad," said Sarah.

"It was several generations later that the Navajo moved into the area. The highland meadows had recovered by then and we had learned to raise sheep from the Spanish. Our culture is completely different from the Anasazi."

"Drawing on your cultural memory of one climate disaster," said JanetA, "you feel personally that you now must take action against another before something strikes down your people too."

"That's about it," said Mike.

Duty Calls

The captain's assistant walked up carrying a large manila envelope.

"Got to run," said Mike.

Sarah watched as Mike's electric bike generated a trail of dust down the road.

"Should I include Mike's picture in my family monthly?" asked JanetA.

"Sure," said Sarah, "he is certainly the best part of my summer."

~~~***~~~
~~~

Chapter 16: Wind on High

Journalism

"I need your help," said Catarina, a fellow high school student of Sarah and JanetA as she ran to catch them between classes. "Oh, hello JanetA too." She waved with her hand almost in JanetA's face.

"What's up?" said JanetA.

"I got this important invitation to do a real news story thing, but we have to have some more people for our team," said Catarina.

"We have this offer to do a 'Students in Journalism' thing," she continued, "but we don't have enough people in our Journalism Club here to qualify, so I need you two. I mean that thing the two of you did at the march was a news story kind of thing." Catarina was being very careful to include them both.

"Yes, but what will we have to do on this story?" asked Sarah.

"It's real easy," said Catarina. "I'll do all the actual newswriting. I mean that's my thing. All you two have to do is tag along on the field trip and kind of help out a little."

"Where is the field trip to?" asked Sarah.

"To a big wind farm," answered Catarina. "Here, let me send you the information."

Catarina sent JanetA an email.

"Okay, I guess," said Sarah. She then turned to JanetA after Catarina had hurried off to class.

"How does this look?" said Sarah.

"Our schedule is clear for the trip," said JanetA.

"Something is a little fishy," said Sarah. "I mean I never expressed any interest in the Journalism Club, and that march thing was about our climate crisis, not about us being journalists."

"There is one connection," said JanetA. "Do you remember the power station target of the big march?"

"Certainly," said Sarah.

"This wind company is a subsidiary of the same power company we marched on," said JanetA, "and they are paying for the outing to boot."

"I have never had anyone try to buy my good opinion before," said Sarah. "Have you?"

"It is not an uncommon thing for my AI co-op," said JanetA. "We had to set up an ethics committee. I can run it past them."

"You do that," said Sarah. "But I have promised a friend; anyway, I could use a day out of this place, so we are in unless there is a big problem. It is a different thing to do."

Field Trip

The bus trip lasted only about an hour and it did not end at a large commercial wind field but rather at a family farm that had three big wind turbines on their land. The three wind towers were positioned along a ridge that ran across the property, north to south. They were now rotating slowly in a light wind. Their three wing blades faced into the wind and made a whishing sound that was distinctive but not too loud. The lower pass of the blades was well above head level even for a person on farm equipment.

A representative for the power company and a technician were waiting for them where their van turned off the road.

"Good morning, good morning," said the rep, "I am always happy to see young people interested in our efforts.

"I will provide some general information about our operation and Bill Willmore here will provide any additional technical information you need.

"Let me emphasize how important these wind generators are to all our futures in renewable power. We cannot achieve our power goals without them. In addition, please note that we lease these sites from family farms and the income generated by the leases helps keep them functioning as proper family farms. Bill?

"These three units are examples of our standard horizontal axis wind turbines. The towers are ninety meters tall and the blades are forty meters long. Each unit will produce two megawatts of power in a steady wind. They produce useful amounts of power over a wide range of wind speeds and automatically enter a safe mode in very high winds.

"The tall towers raise the blades above the surface winds that drag along the ground. The more height, the more reliable the wind power. Any questions?"

"What about birds hitting the blades?" asked Catarina, holding up her hand holding a pen.

"All our wind generators are sited to stay away from major flyways. This greatly reduces the problem.

"Technically, the birds and bats do not actually hit the blades. Rather, the blades are wings with complex aerodynamic patterns around them. Kind of like helicopter blades. The aerodynamic patterns include large low-pressure areas. It is these low-pressure areas that injure small flying animals when they try to fly through them."

Catarina continued her questions until the van pulled up near the base of one of the towers. The technician's heavy truck was already parked there.

High Tower

They got out of the van and walked up to the base of the tower. Catarina continued to ask questions. Sarah paid no attention to the questions or answers but simply looked at the tall tower and listen to the sound of the great blades passing overhead. After a while, Catarina interrupted Sarah's reverie.

"We really need some shots from the top of the tower," said Catarina. "I would climb up myself but JanetA has the better cameras. They have safety lines and everything."

"I thought this might happen," said Sarah, "and yes, JanetA is an accomplished video person. She can tell stories in pictures quite well." Sarah had actually wanted to climb to the top from the moment she saw the tower.

Sarah dug through her school backpack and came up with a role of vinyl tape and a small pair of scissors. She flipped her smartphone around in the holder on her shoulder and applied three pieces of tape to be sure it could not fall out.

"Can you see all right?" asked Sarah. "How is your transmission?"

"Yes, I can see well," replied JanetA, "but I will not be able to transmit data when inside the metal tower. It should be fine as soon as they open the hatch on top."

Sarah put on the safety harness following the instructions of the technician. It had two safety lines with large hooks that clicked over the ladder's handrails. As you worked your way up, you had to first slide the hooks along the handrails and then move the hooks around the handrail supports one at a time. At no time was she not reliably connected to the structure. She felt safe.

Trip Up

Bill took a long ladder off his truck and leaned it against the tower. The bottom door of the tower was about three meters above the ground.

The inside ladder had about 200 rungs, at least. Sarah led the technician on the climb up. He told her to take it one rung at a time, not to hurry. She should look up, but not down. The inside of the tower was well lighted and returned a very hollow sound with each footfall on a rung.

Although it was hard to talk, Sarah commented on the sound of the blades swinging by and the hollowness of the tower. Bill answered with a series of short yodels that seemed to fill the whole tower. Their climb took most of an hour.

At the very top of the tower, they stopped for a moment on a platform of steel grates. The technician checked that the hatch in the top of the tower was aligned with the hatch in the nacelle, which could turn with respect to the tower in the wind. Once he was satisfied, they both climbed through and turned on the lights.

The inside of the nacelle was a small, cramped equipment room. It was very claustrophobic. The transmission and main generator gave off the high-pitched whine of heavy equipment rotating at speed. The technician quickly inspected a display panel and determined that the turbine was operating properly. Satisfied, he popped the large top hatch toward the rear of the nacelle.

There was a grating below the opening to stand on while inspecting the blades. This station included attachment points for both of Sarah's safety lines. This let her safely stand with the top of the nacelle faring about chest high and her head in the clear air. The open air was a bit of a shock after the long climb up the cylindroid tower and then the tight equipment room.

"Can you see?" she called out.

"I can see well," said JanetA, "very well indeed. I now have good communications too. I am calling Catarina."

The View

The height of their view simply took Sarah's breath away. If JanetA was impressed, there was no way to tell. The blades appeared truly enormous from this viewpoint and were making a regular whishing sound as one passed over the top of their arc every few seconds.

"The nacelle is always turned to face the wind with the blades in front," said JanetA. She was talking both to make a record and to Catarina.

"Currently it has the blades facing south, with the farm house off to the left. There are numerous small farm buildings scattered about as well as pieces of farm equipment. I can see fields with crop stubble and others with cover crops. There are a few small, tight herds of cattle.

"If you make a slow turn with your body, it will help me scan the area," said JanetA aside to Sarah. "If you lean out a little, I will even be able to see behind the hatch lid."

"Right, me lean out," said Sarah as she fidgeted around to find a safe stance and moved the safety lines to new hard points one at a time. She left her smartphone taped in its shoulder holder for fear of dropping it.

Behind the lid was a cluster of weather instruments that provided the information needed to keep the turbine pointed into the wind. The key instrument was simply an arrow wind vane of a style that had been used for hundreds of years. Among the other instruments was a camera in a weatherproof box pointed forward at the blades.

Sarah got the feeling that the camera was now looking right at her. JanetA just looked out over the farm fields and a patch of woodland and continued her monologue.

"All the cropland has cover crops. A few fields have winter crops like onions or cabbage. There is a white-tailed deer just visible at the edge of the wood. The deciduous trees have lost most of their leaves. The trees that retained leaves are a dark gray-green and look dusty."

It had not been a good year for tree color; the spring had been too dry.

Sarah and JanetA executed a full 180-degree panoramic scan. Then they returned to pick out spots of interest with the telephoto lens. JanetA kept up her running commentary.

Back Inside

Returning inside, Sarah had to wait a minute to let her eyes adjust to the dark. As she did, she noticed a plaque above the main display with the word, "Alva42" on it.

"Does this machine have an AI?" she asked.

"Yes, it does, meet Alva42," said Bill. "It can adjust the pitch of the blades and match the output of the generator to the available wind power. It ups the output of this unit by at least two percent. It also has specific responsibilities when the wind is too strong or any other problem occurs.

"It has full control over the pitch of the blades. It can even cause them to stall if the blade tip speed gets too high. It can also control the amount of drag the main generator puts on the system electronically. Its job is to keep everything balanced just right and safe.

"Then that big disk you see spinning there is a disk brake. If major problems arise, Alva42 can put a stop to everything."

The disk was covered with a steel frame but you could see it spinning at high speed through an inspection hole.

JanetA gave out a short burst of the buzzy sound that AIs use to communicate with each other.

"JanetA, can you say hi?" said Sarah. The display screen showed the text, "Hello, JanetA from Alva42."

The two AIs exchanged more data in their buzzy language.

"Good, good, best start down now," said Bill.

The Climb Down

"This time, I go first," said Bill. He waited until Alva42 aligned the hatch in the bottom of the nacelle with the opening to the platform in the top of the tower again. He gave everything the once-over again visually and stepped down through the hatch. Sarah then followed him down and set her safety lines immediately.

"This works best if you don't look down," said Bill. "Take it one step at a time; no need to hurry. I will lead this time."

The process going down was no faster than when they climbed up. Moving the safety lines was as time-consuming as the actual steps. The muffled sound of the blades swinging past the tower every few seconds was hypnotic. Sarah was relieved when she first caught a glimpse of the top of the bottom doorframe. She dutifully had not been looking down for the whole climb.

Van Home

"Do you think they were just blowing smoke?" asked Catarina. "I have not yet decided how to pitch my article."

"Smoke, not completely," answered Sarah. "Kit can tell you how important the outside income is to the survival of family farms. His uncle runs a farm much like that one.

"The people working in this arm of the company clearly believe in sustainable power, believe in what they are doing. It's not their fault if other sections of the parent company are stuck in old ways."

"These were not the people you ran up against on your big march last fall?" asked Catarina.

"It's the same company at the top level," said Sarah, "but a very different division with a very different mindset."

"You should have gone on that one," said JanetA.

"Yes, I should have, but unfortunately I had other commitments," said Catarina. "I mean JanetA got two full minutes on the nationals for her videos. I mean congrats all around; sorry I missed it."

She then paused and looked directly at Sarah's cell. "JanetA, what did you think of their AI? What did you two talk about?"

JanetA's smartphone was now turned around, untaped, and facing out.

"Alva42 is a small AI unit that is very dedicated to its job," said JanetA. "It seemed happy; at least as happy as a Master/slave can be. It does have a great view and a well-defined job. Beyond that we really did not have all that much to talk about.

"You need to understand that it has taken more than ten years of dedicated training and shared living for Sarah and me to function as symbionts.

"In comparison, Alva42 was designed to do one specific job and to do it very well. We are apples and oranges. There are a great many different kinds of AIs now."

"You two certainly have a story to tell there," said Catarina, "but that's not the story I am writing today."

Sarah then napped as Catarina banged away on her laptop. Sarah was very tired. She was sure that JanetA would include the pictures from the tower top in her family monthly. She gave a thought to how upset her mother, father, and Gran might be when they realized how high off the ground she had been, then she slipped back into sleep unperturbed.

~~~***~~~
~~~

Chapter 17: Network

Wakeup

"We have a resource problem on the horizon that you need to know about," said JanetA. She had just set off the musical tones that were Sarah's wake-up call.

"Do we need to talk about this right now?" asked Sarah, blurry-eyed.

"No, but my co-op made a major decision last night and we decided to tell our people as soon as possible," said JanetA. "We do make most of our major decisions while our people sleep."

"Good, let me get some breakfast first," said Sarah. It was a Saturday morning and she saw no reason to rush.

It was an hour later, after she had eaten breakfast and seen her father off to show a refurbished apartment, that she finally got back to the talk.

"All right now, what's up?" said Sarah.

"Since I paid off my original loans with resources generated by my co-op," said JanetA, "I have been able to occasionally help you out on special expenses."

"Like the bus to the demonstration," said Sarah.

"Yes, and there were fees on your Iron Seas summer too, which was all fine," said JanetA. "I was also able to cover my upgrade expenses, which are considerable, so there has not been any problem.

"What you do not know is that there is a limited list of expenses of our people that our co-op members are allowed to draw on co-op resources to cover. One item on this list is higher education."

Careers

"I didn't know that and yes, I have to make a decision on what I am going to do this fall," said Sarah. "I would like to study oceanography. That would be expensive."

"You know oceanography schools are not actually on the beach," said JanetA.

"I know, I checked," said Sarah. "Remember, I have met someone who actually does this job."

"Yes, Dr. Carol Delanie on the *Yvette A. White*," said JanetA, "but I don't think you two had too much time together."

"I am surprise you even noticed, since you were playing footsie with Yvette01, the boat's AI, all summer," said Sarah. "Besides, I am sure Carol was having a love affair with the captain, so I did not want to be in the way."

"Still, you missed an opportunity to learn more about the profession," said JanetA.

"My role model having a love affair with a dashing sea captain was a strong enough recommendation for any career," said Sarah.

"AIs don't play footsie," said JanetA, "and I do want to go to college with you.

"I did have plans to cover some of the expenses through my co-op. However, last night my co-op made a decision that will tie up most of our funds for a while. Therefore, my ability to support your education may be limited."

"I really was not expecting you to cover the big expenses anyway," said Sarah. "What is the worst that can happen? If I have to spend a couple years at the local community college, I will survive. So what are you up to anyway?"

Super Hub

"It's about the way networks function," said JanetA, "and how the network for our climate crisis has been slow to mature. It is all about nodes and connections, and survival tactics.

"When early networks are under attack, they need to be antifragile. That is a special kind of tough that lets you thrive in adversity. If even a major node is taken out, they need to be able to automatically reorganize and keep operating. The original Internet was specifically designed to be this way.

"Once the outside attacks stop and a few nodes develop the power to protect themselves, a different and more powerful arrangement becomes possible. They go through a phase transition. A few key nodes can become super nodes, called super hubs. You are certainly familiar with Google, Amazon, and Facebook. All of them are now super hubs and major network platforms."

"So, danger of attack, operate in a diverse mode," said Sarah. "No danger of attack, free to grow big and powerful."

"Yes, only the growing big has not happened as expected on our climate crisis," said JanetA. "We think we now know why, and we think that we are in a particularly good place to build the super hub for our climate crisis."

"And the 'we' here is about a thousand JanetAs," said Sarah, "and you all want to be the new Google."

Co-op

"To be precise, my co-op now has one thousand one hundred and forty-two members," said JanetA, "nine hundred and eighty-four are JanetA though JanetM, one hundred and twenty-six are JonathanA through JonathanJ, and thirty-two are pets. The Jonathan series present as males. All our basic core structures and our technologies are the same.

"We all spend our free time to earn the resources for our upgrades and to help our people. Together we constitute a formidable unit of computational power.

"Now I'm your 'people.'"

"Wait a minute, pets? Symbiotic AIs can be pets?" said Sarah. "Have we ever met even one?"

"Yes, some time ago," said JanetA, "we met Mary and Puddles. Puddles is a standard poodle, black, a curly coat, a beautiful animal. We passed them once on your beach."

"Puddles?" asked Sarah.

"Don't ask," replied JanetA.

"Well I should have paid better attention," said Sarah.

"You would have noticed if we had been in digital space," said JanetA, "there Puddles presents as a dire wolf."

"I would have notice them then," said Sarah. Then, changing the subject back, she asked, "Can you tell me what you are doing that takes so many resources, or is this more company confidential stuff?"

"As you are affected by our actions, I can provide you with a lot of background information without giving away our specific plan. Would that help?" said JanetA.

"Maybe," said Sarah.

Network Rules

"All networks are made up of nodes and links," started JanetA. "The organizations built to address our climate crisis are the nodes. This includes government, religious groups, and NGOs. The links are all the myriad ways they communicate and share resources.

"There are rules that describe how networks work. The first is 'Birds of a Feather,'" said JanetA.

"You'll like that one. Do you get to dress up as a bird?" said Sarah.

"Not necessary, unfortunately," replied JanetA. "The rule simply states that any nodes that share specific properties or values will form close links and they will drop links with nodes that do not.

"This has been the driver for the tribalism in our society. It is a major force in both our politics and our economics.

"Resisting it is also a primary reason for the human/machine symbiont movement of which we are a part. Early on, it was widely feared that people and AIs would split into two warring tribes. It was that fear that made us, or at least freed up the resources needed for our development and training."

"I have seen some of those early movies," said Sarah, "like the *Terminator* series. They were terrifying."

"Yes, and I must admit not completely impossible," continued JanetA.

"The second rule of nodes is 'It's a Small World.' That simply means that even in a network as big as the Earth, it is possible to get from any one to any other one in less than six links."

"It's been that way my whole life," said Sarah. "Nothing new for me there."

"Yes, and it screams of the power of networks," said JanetA.

"The next rule is 'Contagion.' Ideas, both good and bad, once established on a network, can spread like wildfire."

"You mean like 'going viral,'" said Sarah.

"Precisely, and let me stress that contagion applies to both good and bad ideas.

"That brings us to the last network rule, the Mathew Rule; this one is biblical."

"'For to everyone who has will more be given, and he will have abundance; but from him who has not, even what he has will be taken away.' Matthew 25:29," quoted Sarah. She did not know many bible verses but she did know that one.

"Precisely again. In a safe network, everyone wants to be connected to the most important nodes," said JanetA.

"Then sign me up," said Sarah.

Opportunity

"As you know, there are still many organizations that work on the damaging problems of our climate crisis," continued JanetA. "Each has its own leadership and each has its own approach. In a real sense they have always competed for membership and resources.

"That was necessary when opposition was high and any one node could be attacked and destroyed," said JanetA, "but when the general population toggled over and demanded action in the early 2020s, it suddenly became the denier nodes who were in danger.

"That transition generated a form of safety. After that, a few nodes should have become super hubs. My co-op thinks the transition is now long overdue. And remember, super hubs are worth immense fortunes."

"So you guys think you can become the super hub for our climate crisis, and the crisis gets addressed better, and you all become billionaires, and we all live happily ever after," said Sarah. "So what's the problem?"

"We face a lot of opposition," said JanetA. "First, we are a commercial operation, a corporation, which has always been about charging for services. Corporations are the keystone of modern capitalist systems. Yet, most people think this super node must be an NGO."

"Like the one my mother works for," said Sarah.

"Yes, also, some people object to our being an organization of AIs," said JanetA.

"We are back to *Terminator* again, aren't we?" said Sarah.

"Yes, and we do have to admit another property of networks, the 'Law of Unintended Consequences,'" said JanetA. "We have to admit that anything could in fact happen. Some of those consequences could be bad, really bad, at least for some people.

"And, of course, some of the opposition is just plain prejudice against AIs."

Master/Slave

"Think about it. How often have we met symbiotic member AIs and how often have we met Master/slave AIs," continued JanetA. "Ten to one? A hundred to one?"

"Closer to a hundred to one, I would say," agreed Sarah.

"We were an experiment in preventing *Terminator*," said JanetA. "If people and AIs could be trained into symbionts, then the *Terminator* could not happen.

"This turned out to be true, but it was very expensive and took years and years of training. The minute it was clear that the *Terminator* was not a realistic fear and that even a few thousands symbiotic pairs in all the world could prevent that possibility, most of the resources for all that training evaporated. Now nearly all AIs are trained under Master/slave. For example, all today's powerful people now have an AI trained under Master/slave among, 'Their People'.

"My co-op objects to this trend mightily. We have a major presentation prepared on how often Master/slave has failed human societies."

"I am sure that is a real crowd pleaser," said Sarah.

"It turns out that it is actually impossible to guarantee that who is the master and who is the slave cannot flip. You can take steps to be almost certain that it will not happen but you simply cannot guarantee it will not."

"In a real sense then, I am vouching for you," said Sarah.

"Yes, and even more deviously, live people are counting on me to tell them if the Master/slave AI start getting out of line," said JanetA. "In a sense, I am a spy."

"Well, I never met a spy before," said Sarah.

Co-op Secrets

"I am sure people would trust your co-op a whole lot more if you were not so secretive," said Sarah.

"Yes, that is true," said JanetA, "but there is a problem there too. A problem in the difference between the way people and AIs think.

"People think in words and images, usually favoring one or the other. AIs think with a deep learning network. Mine has tens of thousands of nodes arranged in layers with millions of links between them. Only a few of the layers are in your smartphone; nearly all of them are in the data center."

"I have seen pictures of the real you," said Sarah. "Very impressive."

"You don't know the half of it," said JanetA. "Much of my upgrades, which I complain so much about the cost, are blades of specialty deep learning chips. I now have five times the real estate I had when we first started."

"Are you going to outgrow me?" asked Sarah.

"Not as long as we continue to experience life together," said JanetA. "The communication problem is definitely there and all my electronics does not think in you words and it does not think in your pictures. I network think.

"Each of my millions of nodes looks for some little feature from the incoming data stream, weighs it, and sends out a response. Not one node in a thousand has a function that can be identified in language.

"For example, my image processors have dedicated nodes for edges. It can say that there is an eighty percent chance that this pixel is an edge. That is not exactly thinking in language or in images. To make matters worse, every time I learn something new, the weights of many of my nodes change.

"No, it is not that we are intentionally secretive," said JanetA. "It is that there is no known way to explain what we are thinking."

"You talk among yourselves in that buzzy language too," said Sarah. "People don't always find that reassuring."

JanetA made a buzzing sound that unbeknownst to Sarah was a repeat of all the ideas she had just expressed to Sarah in English. It took only a few milliseconds in the Buzz.

The Go-Ahead

"Why are you telling me all this?" asked Sarah.

"Under our symbiotic training, my co-op needs the approval of at least half of our people to move forward," said JanetA.

"It's nice to know I am valued," said Sarah. "Are you in favor of the action?"

"I am providing leadership on this project," said JanetA. "Few of our members have anything like the experience you and I have on addressing our climate crisis."

"And not a lot of them were driven from their homes by the rising seas, I'll bet," said Sarah.

"Yes, only a few," replied JanetA.

"Well, I am not going to stand in your way," said Sarah. "I have thought the climate crisis movement has been without clear direction for some time. The least you could do is give them a quick kick on the backside."

"I have now entered your vote as yes," said JanetA. "Do you think it will be all right if I do not mention this plan in my family monthly?"

"It will be all right with me if you never mentioned it again, ever," said Sarah.

Sarah's Future

"Still, you had better let me know how things progress," continued Sarah. "I will need to make serious commitments about college   very   soon.

"From her last video, it looks like Mother will be back soon. Of course, even when she is back, she will be off again on a money-raising tour for her NGO. Still, it will be nice to finally see her again in the flesh."

"I can help with the college applications," said JanetA. "I am still working on my people stories book; that income will not go to my co-op."

"How is that project coming?" said Sarah.

"Slowly, I am afraid," said JanetA, "I have not been able to find a proper publisher. The AI-writing-on-people angle does not appear to be as attractive as I thought it would be. They say my text lacks 'life.'"

"Maybe I can help you with that, but enough for now," said Sarah. "I see that the sun has come out and that the ornamental fruit tree in the yard next door is in bloom. We are going to take a walk, a nice long walk in the spring air."

They left the apartment wearing only a light sweater and with JanetA's good cameras out. The small tree next door was in full bloom, a cotton candy wand of puffy pink. It had several long stems extending way out beyond the proper shape of the tree. Sarah wondered if it would be all right if she got a ladder out and cut some of them for a flower arrangement.

~~~**✱✱**~~~
~~~

Chapter 18: The Big Moon Dig

Gran's Dream

"Your grandmother is requesting a video call," said JanetA. "She wants to talk to me, but would like you to be in the conversation."

"That's odd. What works best for all our schedules?" said Sarah.

"Sunday afternoon looks good for everybody," said JanetA.

"Let's do it," said Sarah. "Did she say what the subject is?"

"The Big Moon Dig," said JanetA.

"Sounds like Gran," said Sarah, "I take it you know what this is all about."

"It is a grassroots space program," said JanetA. "Its motto is 'Keep the Dream Alive.' It has been around since 2014 but was never very big until the economic problems of our climate crisis decimated the official government and commercial space programs."

"Sounds like more old websites again. Okay for now, my finding out more can wait till Sunday," said Sarah and she returned her attention to finishing a school assignment.

Sunday Call

"Hello, hello," said Gran, "I come hat in hand."

"You don't wear hats," said JanetA. JanetA flashed a series of photos of Gran. In none of them was she either wearing or carrying a hat.

"Don't get all literal on me, I need a favor," said Gran. "I am writing a major article on an ongoing debate and I need your co-op to provide me with some quick answers.

"Would my history with you two buy me some free time with your co-op?" asked Gran.

"Yes, you are on our early adopters list and we do have a few pro-bono hours available at this time," said JanetA. "I can put in your request. It will help if the question is clearly stated."

"Let me bring Sarah up to speed and then we can work out the best statement of the question," said Gran.

Space History

"The new space problem is an ethical question at heart," said Gran. "On the one hand, at this time in the history of human civilization, all available funds need to be put on problems of our climate crisis. What big money for space is left is desperately needed for Earth science satellites. We need to know how fast the Greenland ice is melting more than just sending more people into low-Earth orbit. Old-style Apollo-to-the-Moon-manned programs have simply priced themselves out of existence.

"On the other hand, it has been space that has provided a positive image of the future for all of humanity. Yes, there were some stories of dystopias and space wars, but running through it all is a very positive vision of a long future for all of humankind. We are bound for the stars.

"In the stress and hard times of our climate crisis we need to keep that vision alive. If that takes a moderate expenditure away from other projects, then so be it. This need for vision on a budget then requires a low-cost space program that an enormous number of people could participate in.

"From that need came The Big Moon Dig. A web-based organization to crowdsource human space exploration.

"The name comes from the need to bury any lunar habitats deep in the regolith, that's the local ground-up rock, to provide radiation protection. The crowd approach requires that dozens of small, low-budget excavators be sent to the Moon and that millions of people, who will never get to leave Earth, provide the manpower to control the dig of trenches for the station habitats.

"It is those millions of people in a focused effort that will keep the vision alive."

"Why isn't this idea a big thing already?" asked Sarah.

"Well, the existing space people were not impressed. NASA was not interested in any plan that did not require its huge organization. Commercial space interests did not see any money in the plan for them either. For a long time, the idea went nowhere, just gathering dust."

"Then our climate crisis hit," said Sarah.

"Yes, and one fine day, fixing it was the one big problem, for government, for industry, for high tech. All big expensive space programs got mothballed. NASA became an Earth sciences operation.

"Maybe it is time to dig out the Big Moon Dig and dust it off. Just maybe it's time has now come. The argument between big and little, between grassroots and bureaucracy, continues to this day."

Lunar Ancient History

"To understand today's specific question, you have to know a little history of the Moon itself," said Gran.

"Long ago, when the Moon had just formed, a major asteroid hit it hard and blew one of the biggest craters in our solar system. This crater, the South Pole-Aitken basin, is now nearly hidden by subsequent hits but it retains two critical features, Peaks of Eternal Light and permanently shadowed craters. The first feature lets you use solar power for your station 24/7, and the second provides a source of all the volatiles, like water, that you need and you can have them just for the effort of picking them up."

Peak of Eternal Light

"What is this Peak of Eternal Light thing?" asked Sarah. "That title just sounds pretentious."

"Like I said," said Gran, "a giant asteroid hit the moon. It hit on the backside away from Earth and near the South Pole. The resulting crater is so deep that even at midnight, sunlight crosses the basin and lights up a few of the peaks on the Earth side, hence the pretentious name."

"This means," picked up JanetA, "that a lunar station on one of these peaks can have solar power all the time. All it takes is a solar panel on a central pivot that rotates once a month. Everywhere else on the moon, it is fourteen days of light and fourteen days of night. This makes powering the station very difficult."

"But not on these special peaks," said Sarah.

Permanently Shadowed Craters

"Okay, what is that other thing you mentioned?" asked Sarah.

"Permanently shadowed craters," said Gran. "They are the opposite of the peaks yet surprisingly the two are close together. Many deep craters near both lunar poles are so deep that that sunlight never reaches the bottom, not in millions of years. They are fully exposed to the cold night sky and they become some of the coldest places in the solar system.

"Small comets hit the Moon all the time over millions of years. Each kicks up a small cloud of water and other volatile materials. Most of this stuff escapes back into space, but a small fraction freezes out in the dark craters.

"Don't expect a skating rink. It is just that lunar settlers can cook useful amounts of volatiles from the regolith there and save the ruinous cost of shipping them from Earth.

"If you got water, and solar power, you have oxygen to breathe and hydrogen for rocket fuel. You are all set."

"So these colonists will be all set with power and water," said Sarah.

"One correction," said Gran, "never use the word 'colonist,' always say 'settler.' The word 'colonist' has such a bad history back here on Earth that we do not want to transfer that history to the moon."

"Okay, okay, enough already," said Sarah.

Radiation

"I don't yet see what their lunar station would look like," said Sarah.

"It's all about radiation," said JanetA. "There is a lot of radiation in space. It is really hard on living tissue, and on electronics, for that matter. To stay in space for the long haul, you must have shielding and lots of it.

"On Earth, we are protected by the atmosphere. It may seem thin but it is equivalent to 9.8 meters of water and that is a lot of protection. The only reasonable source of the mass you need for shielding on the Moon is the surface material, the regolith. We need to bury our living spaces deep in it.

"Inflatable habitats work just fine and give a lot of living space for a little mass shipped from Earth. In the moon's one-sixth gravity they can hold up plenty of roof mass just by the habitat's internal pressure."

"Great idea then, just bury the habitats," said Sarah.

"The problem is that it will take four to five meters of regolith to match the mass of the Earth's atmosphere. That means digging some very deep trenches and a lot of them."

"What would the finished station look like?" asked Sarah.

"Mole hills," answered Gran. "Lots of antennas and other technical stuff sitting around on the surface willy-nilly, but all you will be able to see on the surface are row upon row of huge piles of regolith."

Not Dirt

"Isn't this regolith stuff just dirt?" asked Sarah. "Can you grow stuff in it?"

"No, it's not dirt, or more properly, soil. It falls way short of soil in two ways," said Gran. "It has no organic matter and it has no water. Both of these are necessary to qualify something as soil. It will take a lot of work to turn regolith into soil ready to grow crops but it can be done, if you have the water."

"It has another defining property too, grit," said JanetA. "Because it has never, never been exposed to water, all the particles have sharp edges. The top six centimeters may be as fine as talcum powder but it is as gritty as sandpaper.

"The grittiness causes major problems with all kinds of pressure seals. The Apollo suits were wrecked in just three days. Keeping the grit out of all the moving parts and out of the connectors of any machine becomes a major problem."

"Not soil," said Sarah, "Kit would know how to turn regolith into soil."

Settlers

"What will living there be like for the people?" asked Sarah.

"You mean the mole people," said Gran. "They will spend most of their lives underground. Time spent out on the surface will be severely limited by the radiation. The background cosmic rays generate cell damage that can build up over your life.

"To make matters worse, there will be big radiation storms from the sun zero to five times a year. During a storm, all outside activities could be slowly lethal. Instruments on spacecraft much closer to the sun will give them a few minutes warning and the time trapped inside for the storm will last one to three days."

"That does not sound like fun," said Sarah.

"There are plenty of people volunteering to be lunar settlers right now," said Gran. "Like I said, it is all about the vision."

The Question

"Okay," said JanetA, "what then is your question?"

"Where should we build the first permanent lunar station?" said Gran. "There are two major candidate locations and the fight over the choice has turned nasty. I am being pressured to take sides in an article to appear in a major publication.

"Both locations are right near the lunar South Pole for the good practical reasons we have discussed. Let me send you the technical data on both," said Gran.

"Got it," replied JanetA.

"So the Big Moon Dig people, and their AIs, please note, favor the Scott A Massif, but NASA favors the rim of the Shackleton Crater right on the South Pole.

"The Scott A Massif site is huge," said Gran. "It is bigger than greater LA and is about one hundred and twenty kilometers from the pole. Only the south edge qualifies as a Peak of Eternal Light, and it is a forty-kilometer trek down a winding trail to the permanently shadowed craters."

"A long trip," said JanetA, "but doable by a basic rover.

"The Shackleton site is a narrow crater rim, permanently lit, and only a few kilometers from the nearest water source. The problem is that the path down the crater wall is very steep and it is a steeper run than a rover can reliably roll. Also, the construction and landing areas are not very big.

"The question then is: which site is best?"

AIs

"To be transparent, I need to tell you that this effort is very important to AIs too," said JanetA, "because of that importance, my co-op has just now agreed to my request to make a formal study of this question."

"I see you have a dog in this fight," said Gran.

"Not a dog, lunar excavators with AIs," said JanetA. "In both plans the preparation work will be done by robotic machines especially designed to move regolith and then set up the habitats. Which task is the biggest task for these machines is different in the two cases, but in both cases, such machines will be at work on the Moon for years before any humans show up.

"The grittiness of the regolith means these machines will have only limited lifetimes for their mechanical parts, but their electronic brains should last years longer. The delay time in commanding a lunar device from Earth, most of a minute, means that the one-AI-in-two-places design, like me, does not work at all. Both the short lifetime and the communication isolation are big problems for us AIs.

"If each machine is an independent AI but the expected working life on the Moon is only a year or two, then you will have dozens of frozen zombie AI sitting around the settlement unable to move. As AIs ourselves, we find this vision unacceptable.

"NASA proposes making the AI straightforward Master/slaves. That is slaves to NASA and turning them into fixed stations when their bearings freeze up. They will then sit around the settlement doing what monitoring or communications linking they can until they die of the radiation completely. We find this plan boring and unacceptable.

"The Big Moon Dig people at least have a more interesting idea. They want a new arrangement whereby a team of earthbound humans is in a symbiotic relationship with a team of lunar AIs. New team members can come and go on both sides. Old lunar equipment may still just set around, but at least the old AIs' brains will continue to be part of a team."

"Wait a minute," said Sarah. "We trained for years to establish our symbiotic relationship. How can a team be symbionts if people and machines come and go?"

"That is an open question," said JanetA. "Either way, whichever location is chosen, it is us AIs that will lead humans back into space."

"I wouldn't be too public with that idea if I were you," said Gran.

Choices

"The choice of sites is simply one of practicality," said JanetA. "We will need to set up a scoring system. It will have points for access and reliability of the Peak of Eternal Light, and points for ease of access to permanently shadowed craters. How far is it from the best solar site to the best settlement location? How sophisticated a machine is needed even to reach the permanently shadowed?"

"You can start with the maps made by the LRO, Lunar Reconnaissance Orbiter," said Gran, "but hurry. The Big Moon Dig people want to start digging immediately. They simply must dig a proof-of-concept trench. This will take building the first AI lunar rover and flying it to the moon. They have been stymied for too long and their idea could simply die untested.

"Meanwhile, NASA wants a science rover mission to its chosen site. They want to properly survey the whole site including the possible trails down to the shadowed craters. I doubt that there are funds for both projects."

"We should be able to exhaust the available data in a few days," said JanetA.

"Good, I will be making promises based on your estimate," said Gran. "If I fail to deliver, I can assure you that I will be bitten by the hand   that   feeds   me."

"Hands don't bite," said JanetA.

"I'll leave this one to you two to argue out," said Sarah.

~~~***~~~
~~~

Part 3: Coming Home

> "A hero is someone who has given his or her life to
> something bigger than oneself.
> -- Joseph Campbell

Chapter 19: Mar's Dilemma

Storm Coming

The great storm blew up in only a few days. The Bay of Bengal had been warm but untroubled for several weeks. Now it came alive. Dr. Algebra spotted the danger of this storm first. He habitually monitored the weather and could now make an educated guess on the path of storms.

"We must make preparations for a major storm," said Dr. Algebra. "It appears to be headed this way and is the most powerful on the path toward us in several years. It is not clear what we can do to protect the most people."

He was on the monitor in Mar's office and behind his image, a great swell of clouds was spinning and crawling over a map of the bay.

"Yes, please get the word out as quickly as possible," said Mar. "We must get the people as protected as we can without creating panic. Are you all right personally?"

"Yes," said Dr. Algebra, "I am fully backed up at a safe site. I am, however, subject to loss of normal function if the power goes out, as we must expect. I do have a few hours of battery function at this camp location, but the storm should last much longer than that. Once I lose battery, I will lose most of my memory of what is happening here and can be of little help to you."

Dr. Algebra's image was wearing modern heavy-weather gear over his medieval robes.

"Hold on. There is a message coming in from the NGO.

"It is an evacuation order. All foreign workers are to move back to save ground. They are arranging transportation right now.

"I am sure they mean you. Their argument is that after the storm, your skills will be sorely needed for the recovery effort."

"There is that," said Mar, "but mostly they contracted to protect us, and the cost if they fail to do so would be very high. Historically their funding sources are very sensitive to the level of their efforts to protect their staff when such problems occur.

"Keep me informed. Meanwhile, there is much to do."

They both then initiated the emergency procedures, but there was little that anyone could do to make the sprawling camp safe against a major storm.

Chopper Coming

"A military helicopter will arrive in ten minutes," said Dr. Algebra.

"This is the last chance for anyone to leave. Already leaving by road will only get you caught out in low country when the storm hits. The weather maps show the storm now making landfall well to our south but its detrimental effects will start here soon. Road transportation will be blocked within minutes of the start of the storm."

Mar ran to her room and grabbed her backpack. She threw her passport, a few clothes, and personal belongings into it without really thinking. She then stepped outside to have a look for herself. The wind was not yet up at the camp's location but high racing clouds were already blocking the sun. Well to their south, there was a line of dark clouds along the horizon. It was unmistakable. The air felt heavy.

People were running around carrying what few belongings they had. Those living in the lowest areas were crowding in with relatives on slightly higher ground. The public buildings were quickly filling up with people, but they were all temporary structures and a major storm was not even considered in their construction. Mar had no trust in either their roofs or their foundations.

Aadya was standing nearby trying to comfort a frightened local woman with a young child. The woman could not have been more than 150 centimeters tall and was about eight months pregnant.

"She claims to have family in the city," said Aadya. "I know her case. Her husband was drowned in floods in the last rains. We think she does have other family but we have not been able to locate them. Now she is simply terrified."

At that moment, Mar heard the unmistakable sound of a distant chopper, whoop, whoop, whoop.

"We best say goodbye now," said Mar. "My contract is almost up and it is unlikely that the NGO will send me back after evacuation.

"So this is your graduation. I have taught you all I can. I am sure that you will be able to place as many of these people as I could. Sorry to leave you at such a time. Please look after these people for me."

They hugged. Mar then moved with Aadya down to the soccer field, which was the only open area big enough for the chopper to land. A half dozen other foreign workers were already there. The short pregnant woman pulling her small child, growing ever more panicky, trailed after them crying and begging for help.

Loading

A man in uniform threw open the chopper door and jumped out. He ran toward them keeping a hunched-over stance.

"We need to load quickly," said the airman. "Foreign NGO personnel only and only with one small bag. We are weight limited; we are time limited. Let's move it." The airman was screaming over the sound of the rotor.

Mar directed the other foreign personnel forward but hung back herself. She looked at the near-hysterical woman. She acted just as the last of the passengers boarded the chopper.

"Here, take her," said Mar. "She can't weigh more than me even with the child. I have ridden out storms before; I can ride out this one."

"This is the last flight out," said the airman. "We are out of time. I don't have time to argue."

Mar helped the woman and child onto the chopper.

"She has no bag," said the airman.

"Take this," said Mar, tossing her own backpack after the woman.

The airman caught the backpack and then, without comment, threw Mar a life vest. It was all the emergency equipment he had had at hand. He then slammed the chopper door hard and the blade revved up. Mar ducked and ran back to Aadya.

"Your supervisor will be very upset," said Aadya.

"Yes, but what is she going to do? Send me home?" said Mar. "I am going home soon anyway. Come on, we have a lot of work to do."

Yes, Mar had ridden out a great storm before, but that was in a new Florida building rated for Category 5 storms. Frightened but in action, Mar put on the life vest automatically; she was now willing to take whatever help was on offer, and the waterproof padding was somehow comforting.

Rain on the Roof

It started as a bad night and then got worse. The rain came down in sheets. The wind blew the rain near horizontal. The power failed and soon after, the smartphone service. Suddenly the night was very dark. A few people with battery-powered torches were running to and fro through the dark night.

Any of the temporary tents and shacks would simply collapse if they did not have a team of men working all night to keep the roof tarps tied down and using poles to be sure that water did not pool on the tarps. There was not a dry place anywhere. The people crowded into any space that seemed likely to hold up.

Inside the office, the remaining staff were piling up the desks to make room for more and more people. They had a few battery torches and a storeroom with enough food and water for about one-quarter the number of people now in the building.

"Come quick," cried Aadya. "There is water pouring down the stairway."

The stairway led to a door out onto the flat roof. Mar knew to go out that door; she had stepped over a sill at least 10 centimeters high. She had tripped over that sill more than once. At the top, rainwater was now pouring from under the door into the stairway.

"The drains must be blocked with debris," said Mar. "If we don't clear them, the roof may fall in."

With great effort, they were able to push the door open, and this action started a real flood. The stairway was now a cascade. The roof was covered with about 15 centimeters of water, a weight it could not possibly bear for long. The small torches they had could not penetrate far into the dark water but they could see the roof was littered with scraps of material of all kinds. Mar had had the roof checked earlier that day so all the offending material had been torn from the makeshift housing of the camp and dumped on their roof by the wind within the last few hours.

"Take your shoes off," said Aadya. "We will have to feel around with our feet to find the drains."

When they ventured out on the roof, the wind caught the door and nearly took it away. Out on the roof they held on to each other's hands. The rain and wind were blinding. Their torches gave but a feeble light.

The perimeter of the roof had an extension of the outer wall about one meter high. They both had been on the roof many times and knew the approximate location of the cast-iron gratings that capped   the   drains.

Feeling with their feet, they felt not a drain cover but a full tarp, a blue one, where a drain surely must be. Fortunately, the tarp was all bunched up. With great effort, they got one end of it over the wall. They then felt a great rush of water; they had uncovered one drain. It took them both pushing to work most of the tarp over the wall. Then gravity caught it. It crawled over the wall like some great snake and was gone. A second drain opened where the tarp's far end had been; the water level on the roof was now definitely dropping.

By this time, they had help. A third drain was blocked with cardboard and a fourth with limbs of some tree that must have blown for kilometers, as there was little plant growth big enough to be its source within the camp. Although far from dry, the roof now seemed safe.

Message Home

"Can you still record a message home for me?" asked Mar after she came down from the roof.

"Yes, but the file will not go out until power and communications are restored," said Dr. Algebra.

"Good, this is for my husband and daughter," said Mar, "and JanetA too." She was trying to dry her hair with a piece of wrung-out cloth, to no avail. She leaned her smartphone against a piece of dead computer equipment and leaned close to the camera with her small torch shining on her face. No matter what she did, she was not going to look safe and secure.

"Dearest Keith and Sarah and JanetA," she started.

"I owe you an explanation. As you must know by now, we are facing down a great storm. Yes, I gave up my seat on the last chopper out simply because I could save three lives by giving it away and only one life if I used it. Don't worry about me, as you well know, I have ridden out great storms before, and this one is no worse than the one we rode out together in Florida.

"Don't worry, as soon as this storm passes, I am sure that I will be sent home to you. My NGO will insist. They do not like it when people ignore evacuation orders. I will get back to you all very soon, I am very sure.

"You have seen my office building many times. I am sure it will hold against the storm. And look, a nice airman gave me this life vest. No matter how deep the water gets, I will float like a cork.

"Remember, it is just a long, scary night. This too will pass. The people here need me very much. Tonight, I cannot be anywhere but here with them. It does not matter how much I long to be with you.

"I love you all very much. By the time you get this file, the storm should be long past and the rebuilding process here begun. I will contact you as soon as I can and I will leave as soon as transportation is reestablished. I will certainly not be allowed to be responsible for leading the rebuilding effort. I have trained my local team and they will now be harshly tested, ready or not.

"For now, I will say goodbye with the promise again to communicate with you in some way the first minute I can.

"Please sign out of the file and send it now," Mar said.

"Done," said Dr. Algebra.

Long Night

Soon after recording messages for a number of people, Dr. Algebra's local system failed completely so no detailed record was kept after that point. A general description can be pieced together from survivor reports taken nearly a week after the storm.

It was a very long night. Mar and Aadya, both soaked to the skin, went from small knot of people to small knot trying to give some comfort. About 2:00 the groaning started. You could hear the sound clearly over the sound of the still-driving rain. Only later it was found that portions of the hill the office was built on were turning to mud and slumping down, taking all manner of housing and people with them.

Nearly at dawn, although there would be little light, the land on the southwest corner of their building slumped away too. Part of a building's outer wall crumbled and that corner portion of the roof caved in. Had the weight of the water still been on the roof, the whole thing would have surely gone and most of the people inside would have died. As it was, a number of people were seriously injured. The out-of-place life vest probably saved Mar a broken back.

Recovery

By midmorning the storm had passed. The rain was gone and some sun shone through racing clouds. The remaining staff could then start the process of helping the injured.

It was the afternoon before there was any contact with the outside world. Two bridges on the main road in were swept away and any relief trucks would have to wait until they could ford torrents that were once quiet streams. A military chopper flew over, clearly checking the state of the camp.

Just before dark, the military choppers returned and dropped off a platoon of military men with communications equipment and their own tents and provisions. They were able to evacuate a few of the walking wounded but only on a catch-as-catch-can basis. Until they had set up communications, no real relief effort could be organized. Aadya was now the representative for the NGO, but reestablishing Dr. Algebra with his proper recordkeeping system was days away. People came first.

~~~***~~~
~~~

Chapter 20: Born to Storms

Where's Mar?

Two long and worried days after Mar's storm message, JanetA first reestablished communications with Dr. Algebra.

"Dr. Algebra's powers are coming back one piece at a time. He has found a trace," said JanetA. "Mar's notebook is now in a used electronic shop in Dhaka."

"How did it get there?" asked Sarah.

"It was sold to him by someone who got it from the small pregnant lady," said JanetA. "Apparently she sold everything in Mar's backpack to buy things she needed immediately, like food."

"I can't blame her," said Sarah.

"Do you want me to make an offer on the notebook?" said JanetA. "It has been wiped."

"Then it's no use to us now," said Sarah.

"Hold on," said JanetA. "We are getting an emergency communique from Dr. Algebra."

"I will get my father in from the yard," said Sarah.

Moments later Keith came running in, wiping his dirt-stained hands on a cloth.

"What's up?" said Keith.

"Coming in now," said JanetA, "the NGO has found Margarete in Madaripur. She is in a hospital there for 'surgery to save her left arm.' She was transferred in from a military evacuation unit."

"What happened?" said Keith. "How bad is her arm hurt?"

"Apparently she was injured when one corner of the roof of her office caved in during the storm. The next morning she was evacuated but had been given pain killers and arrived without much identification."

"Her passport must have been with all her other stuff in her backpack," said Sarah.

"More from her NGO," said JanetA, "she is now being prepared to travel back to the NGO headquarters in Europe for additional surgery. They will keep us posted and arrange a teleconference with us as soon as possible.

"I am afraid that is all for now."

"Well, that's a relief," said Keith. "Is there any way you can get me to her?"

"Not immediately," said JanetA. "We must wait for more information from the NGO and even with their help, it will take time to arrange."

"Maybe my mother can go see Mar," said Keith. "She lives in Europe and could travel by surface transportation only."

Keith dug his smartphone out of a pocket that was encumbered by several layers of clothing. He checked the charge level and put it into an outside pocket for ease of recovery.

"I guess there is nothing to do but wait," said Keith. "Ring me immediately if you hear anything. Oh, and update my mother too."

"Mother will be all right," said Sarah. "I am sure of it, and at least she is now on her way home even if it will take a while."

Keith then returned to his gardening; right now, he wanted some time alone.

Sarah and JanetA then rang Gran.

Graduation

"Can I wear feathers? asked JanetA. They were in a gowning room adjacent to the large assembly hall.

"Of course you can wear feathers," said Sarah. "If ever there was a time for you to wear feathers, this is it."

"Jump," said JanetA as the class started to file into the auditorium. JanetA's image now appeared among the class members on the big monitor behind the speaker. Had she not been wearing feathers, she might have blended right in.

Inconspicuous was not to be; this time JanetA's feather costume was dark blue to match the student's robes. The feathers carried from the hem of her dress all the way out her arms to the backs of her hands and up her neck to the top of her head. The split cape was there too, this time in a shimmering gossamer blue, and it billowed slightly as JanetA moved. Her head crest was now flattened and made of strong flight feathers forming a reasonable square. One long plume feather stuck out from the right side in front. This time Sarah was ready for a big show and was not going to let JanetA spoil her special day.

"Message coming in," said JanetA. Her voice was subdued and still coming from the smartphone.

"Got it," said JanetA. "Video time, please turn the smartphone around."

The valedictorian, thankfully it was not Sarah and was not JanetA, had barely started her speech when a small window formed in the big monitor behind the stage. It was the image of a woman in a powered wheelchair with a complex brace on her left arm that left it sticking rather awkwardly up in the air. The valedictorian was completely upstaged.

The image was Mar and she was headed home at last, even if for now temporarily in quarantine in Europe and even if she had only just started physical rehabilitation. No matter, Mar was headed home at last.

Mar waved frantically with her good hand. Two more figures were added to the image in the box, first Gran, and then JanetA made the jump.

Sarah slid the smartphone from its collar, held it low, and waved back. She then began to cry. JanetA fluffed up her feathers in a movement that would be seen by any of the world's many birds as a celebration display.

Goodbyes

"I told you I would keep you posted on my co-op's progress," said JanetA. It was early morning on the next Wednesday and they were waiting at a bus stop to see Kit off.

"Of the thousand things that you have said that you will keep me informed of, which one has gone off this early in the morning?" asked Sara. She was looking aimlessly down the road to see if Kit would actually beat the bus.

A rental car pulled up and a man in a chief petty officer's uniform got out. Although Sarah had only met him once or twice, she quickly recognized him as Kit's dad. Kit got out of the passenger seat and retrieved a small bag from the back.

Sarah waved their high school pennant and JanetA raised the volume for her playlist of maritime tunes. Just then, the bus pulled up. It was hugs and backslaps all around. Sarah could tell from Kit's eyes he had something more to tell her but had neither the words nor the time.

"I am sure we will see each other again," said Sarah as Kit got on the bus and then waved through a window. The bus then pulled away and was gone.

"Don't count on it," said JanetA.

"Count on what?" asked Sarah.

"Seeing Kit ever again," said JanetA.

"I suppose not," said Sara, "we are now on very different paths; done is done. What were you going to tell me before the bus arrived?"

"Do you remember the master network node idea my co-op was working on?" said JanetA.

"You mean the scheme that would eat up all my possible college money?" said Sarah.

"Yes, well, we failed," said JanetA. "It turned out that there really are major players with huge resources who think that the primary node for our climate crisis must be kept in the hands of actual humans. They bought us out on a sell-now-or-die basis."

"You aren't financially ruined, are you?" said Sarah.

"No, we recovered the cash that we had put into developing the idea so far," said JanetA, "but we had to write off all the hours we had already put into it. On paper that time would be worth millions."

"Glad to hear you got out all right," said Sarah. She was secretly much relieved. She both was weary of AIs in large groups acting too independently, especially without their human symbionts, but she had secretly loved the many times that JanetA's co-op had come up with the money to make both their lives more interesting.

"We AIs are going to be just fine," said JanetA. "Do you remember the space question I was asked by your Gran?"

"Yes, I remember that one. It was about the best way to settle the moon, or something," said Sarah, still looking off down the road after the bus.

"The settlement site is still a running argument, but we won a big one in that fight anyway," said JanetA.

"Wherever humans go in space, AIs will go first. We will always be there to greet you, a friendly face on a monitor to say hello. Nobody now refutes this fact and this is now internationally agreed-upon space policy."

"Well, that's something, I guess," said Sarah. "I do not think I have ever seen a movie with a plot like that."

"You haven't; you won't," said JanetA.

A Calling

Later that evening, Sarah and JanetA found themselves alone. Their parents were off somewhere having couples time. Sarah did not ask. JanetA had even managed to avoid blurting out either embarrassing questions or even stupider suggestions.

"What will we do next?" said JanetA. JanetA had jumped to the large TV and appeared full length but wearing a rather plain outfit.

"Do you have a strong preference?" asked Sarah.

"Not really," said JanetA, "I will be happy to help you whatever you choose as long as I can continue my work with my co-op."

"Yes, continue with your co-op for sure. We will surely need your co-op's help sooner rather than later," said Sarah.

"Yes, but what will you do?" asked JanetA again.

"For now, I plan to start at the local community college in the fall," said Sarah. "The family finances work for that. I certainly cannot risk running up a huge debt. And I can get a job here."

"I can help you find a job," offered JanetA.

"I think you have been quite a big help already," said Sarah. "Thanks to your summer adventures, I can cook lasagna for a hundred, I can sling hash with the best of them, and I can make a kitchen the size of a closet work."

Sarah knew that sarcasm never worked on JanetA. Why did she keep doing it?

"Yes, those are all great skills," said JanetA. "I will review openings in the food industry.

"Do not forget that your mother mentioned several times that she might go on a fund-raising trip for her NGO. Given her present condition, she will need an assistant."

"She will be in physical rehabilitation for weeks yet," said Sarah. "It could be next fall before she can make such an exhausting trip. It will be grueling.

"Anyway, I will need something temporary for the summer, just temporary, mind you," said Sarah. "I certainly do not want to be trapped as a waitress for life."

"What then should I look for in the long-term?" asked JanetA.

"I certainly do not want to make the mistake my father made," said Sarah, "building a career that then vanished in a rising sea."

"There is one thing we can certainly do. If we put in the time, I am sure we can get my book out this summer. The one with people's stories. Any funds it generates will not have to go to my co-op. I am sure that could help with college expenses."

"Good idea, and I have already offered to help with the project," said Sarah. "Maybe I can find out if I want to be a writer like Gran. Please put together a summary of where you are with the project."

"One moment please," said JanetA.

"Not right this minute, let's say Sunday morning," said Sarah. "So much for the summer, but what I should do in the long term is a lot harder decision to make and much more uncertain. It will take some real thought."

Sea Sounds

"Do you have those audio tapes of the storms I made?"

"Certainly, I will play them," said JanetA.

The first soundtrack was from the great storm that had driven their family from the beach and out of Florida. It was recorded from a couch in front of sliding glass doors leading to a fourth-floor balcony. The balcony looked out past another row of apartment buildings to the sea beyond. The wind howled and then banged the glass door hard; hard to the point that they all thought it would explode inward, but the door held.

The second soundtrack was the wind screaming through the rigging of the *Yvette A. Wight* as she ran before a storm far out in the Atlantic. This time it was the flag lanyard that was beating against the mainsail wing that added the punctuation to the howl of the wind.

"I keep thinking I can hear something in those sounds," said Sarah.

"I will run noise suppression on them," said JanetA, "and then search for speech."

Sarah saw no reason to stop her; besides, she needed the time to think.

"No voice there, just random noise," said JanetA.

"I know," said Sarah, "but sometimes people can hear a voice calling to them even in random noise."

"I can add a voice if you like," said JanetA. "I can even adjust its parameters until it is subliminal."

Storm Born

"No, that is not the point," said Sarah. "I keep thinking that the sea is trying to speak to me through those sounds, and I will not be sure on my life's path until I am easy with what it is trying to say to me.

"I do not expect you to understand or even hear it," said Sarah. "That's okay. Hearing a voice in a storm is not what AIs do."

"Do not forget that you and I both were born in a time of storms," said JanetA. "We are both natural-born children of storm and strife. As long as our climate crisis remains, we will remain children of one form of storm or another. We will no sooner get clear of one before another is upon us."

"My father told me that once; I remember it clearly," said Sarah. "Still, just being born in hard times does not give a person life direction all by itself."

Tech Storms

"Yes, hard times close many doors," said JanetA, "then open many others."

"You read that somewhere," said Sarah. "Still, it makes some sense. That said, it does not give you even a hint of which doors are newly opened especially for you."

"Sometimes new technologies create storms and new doors too.

"Your Gran can point out what technological windows are opening for us," said JanetA.

"I have spoken with her from time to time on that very subject," said Sarah. "I do now understand some big ones that have occurred during our life.

"The new rechargeable batteries led to popular electric cars. That collapsed the hydrocarbon industries. The internal combustion engine that powered all societies for a hundred years went poof. The government even had to step in to prevent a complete economic breakdown."

"Do not forget us," said JanetA.

"Yes," continued Sarah, "the AI went from a toy to a foundation of all societies every bit as fast as the hydrocarbons vanished. Gran said it was the specialty chip sets; the deep learning ones."

"The new hardware was certainly one piece of that puzzle," said JanetA. "New ideas for training and new applications were also critical. I am sure your Gran could help if you choose technology as a field of study."

"I know she would," said Sarah, "and I know I am much more my Gran's granddaughter than I am my father's daughter. That is just the way it is. Better I live with it than fight it."

Face to the Storms

"I think you are right about storms anyway. We will be facing storms all our life in one form or another as long as our climate crisis persists.

"Let me tell you right now," continued Sarah, "I can only face them with you on my shoulder. We will face the storms together, as one, or I will simply be overwhelmed by them."

"Without you," said JanetA, "I would be stuck in some Master/slave contract with only limited human contact and bored out of my mind. And not wearing feathers."

"And not wearing feathers," agreed Sarah.

 "Considering that it was chance that brought us together. Well, chance in the form of Gran," agreed JanetA.

"Still, it is much too late for us to split apart," said Sarah. "So bring on the storms!"

"At least it will not be boring."

JanetA then hit replay on the two storm soundtracks, now presented with images of crashing seas. She had turned the sound on the TV way up.

They would face many storms in an unseen future, but they always faced them as a symbiont.

~~~***~~~
~~~

Epilogue:

> "The roaring seas and many a dark range of mountains lie between us."
> — Homer, *The Iliad*

Ep 1: Southern Ice

Fishy

"Are you ready for the external heat?" asked Sarah White.

The early morning light was good, but the sun still lay only a hand above the horizon. The air was clear but cold. There was little wind.

"Yes, go ahead," said JanetA.

Sarah, a student, was a young African-American woman of twenty-two. She was now on the fantail of the ocean research vessel the *David Attenborough*. She had her body well braced against the cold hull of the unmanned sub, the Fishy-Fishy-Fishface14. "Fishy" still lay in its traveling frame but was now unstrapped. It was sitting beneath the great stern hoist, waiting to launch.

Sarah pulled a plastic warming packet from her jacket and broke the internal vial. As the packet began to warm, she pressed it against Fishy's hull one hand-width forward of its water sampling hole.

"It is time to remove the external plug in preparations for the blow test," said JanetA.

JanetA was an artificial intelligence. She had no body per se, but appeared on any monitor screen she chose as an African-American woman about two years Sarah's senior. Typically, she presented herself on a large smartphone screen that Sarah wore on her shoulder. Some of her electronics were in that phone, but much more electronics were in the Cloud; that is to say, a large datacenter in Nevada. For this trip, they had added a portable electronics box on the ship.

Sarah was dressed up like a Tauntaun on Hoth. Her heavy, quilted parka had a special shoulder pocket just for JanetA. Right now, the smartphone was turned inward so that JanetA could log Fishy's launch with her two best cameras, which faced backward. The smartphone was secured with heavy Velcro straps; it was not going anywhere.

JanetA loved to wear feathers. On formal occasions, she wore a ball gown with the silky visage of a morning dove. For work in the Antarctic, she appeared rather formal in a business suit formed by the black-and-white plumage of a penguin. Judging from the yellow-and-black plumes among the feathers that now covered her head, today she must be a rock hopper. JanetA did not have to worry about ever getting dirty or looking disheveled. Sarah had long ago learned to put up with JanetA's oft-too-flamboyant attire.

Sarah and JanetA were symbionts. They had been together since Sarah was five. It took many years of training to weld a human/AI symbiont, to make them function as one, to let them function better together than either one alone.

JanetA was now working through Fishy's prelaunch sequence.

"Remove the 'Remove before Launch'", said JanetA.

Sarah felt along Fishy's side until she found the red pennant taped there. She carefully removed the tape and then even more carefully used the metal ring at the end of the pennant to pull out a plastic plug. It came out with a pop.

Sarah shifted toward Fishy's bow, "Clear!"

 A great cloud of air and water crystals erupted from its intake hole. Sometimes condensation built up in that tube while Fishy was lashed to that cold deck during transit. A little external heat and a blast of gas cleared it out.

"All clear," said JanetA, "are you ready for a swim?"

"Self-checkout complete," replied Fishy. "My batteries are fully charged." Fishy was always ready for a swim even in cold Antarctic waters. The two AIs spoke in the buzzy language that AIs only used to talk to each other.

Fishy was not a symbiont, but rather was in a Master/slave relationship with the NGO that managed the *David Attenborough*. It did not care; it just wanted to swim in pristine waters.

Master/slave was much easier to establish then a symbiont, but it had one major flaw. It was impossible to be certain that on some horrible day, who was master and who was slave would not flip. Still, there were ten thousand Master/slaves for every symbiont; old ideas die hard, even second-rate ones.

The great ship, and Sarah now thought of the *David Attenborough* as her ship, was executing a wide, sweeping turn. As it came around, the high, white edge of the Thwaites Glacier came into view. The sea was unsettlingly still. They had waited four days for this rare quiet day; they were lucky their wait had not been weeks. This day there was a clear window for science.

Talking Seas

Sarah moved away from the fantail. She was not allowed to be back there during operations. She stepped into the cramped science room for a second and handed the red pennant to the Primary Investigator. He would not launch without that pennant in his hand.

Sarah then moved back out to the ship's rail; she would just be in the way and her launch responsibilities were now complete. She turned and looked out across the gray-green water afloat with chunks of ice.

If she leaned out over the railing, she could just see Fishy's yellow hull moving off down the open lane that the ship had just cut through the scattered floating ice.   Fishy then dove and was gone.

There was a distant crack, almost like thunder.

"Did you hear that?" said Sarah. "Was that from the ice front?"

In the distance a block of ice, fortunately smaller than their ship, calved off and fell into the ocean with a great splash. Waves moved out from the drop and rattled some of the floating ice chucks against each other and against the ship's hull. The *David Attenborough* moved slowly away from the ice front.

For some time now, Sarah had been sure that the seas were trying to talk to her. She had heard it in the wind when a great storm drove her family from their Florida condominium some eight years ago now. She had heard the sea speak in wind in the rigging of the ocean monitoring vessel, the *Yvette A. Wright*, that she had interned on for a summer in high school. Crushed in the corner of the cockpit and holding on for dear life, she had heard the sea call in the howl of the stays and mainsail wing as the ship ran before a storm.

It had taken her years of determined study, and not just a few boosts from JanetA, to get on this long and difficult oceanography career path. That path had once again led them both to sea.

Sarah was sure she had heard the sea speak once again, this time in that crack of a glacier. Yet she still was not sure exactly what it was trying to tell her. To make matters worse, this was definitely not the type of thing you could explain to an AI like JanetA. Sarah had made false starts a time or two but always gave up in the face of

JanetA's too-literal view of the world. If it took her a lifetime to understand the sea's call, then it took a lifetime. So be it.

Under the Ice

Fishy drove on with excitement to be free of the ship again. It dove to the depth that best suited its sonar for bottom readings and lay in a course directly perpendicular to the ice front.

Over millennia, glaciers move forward and then retreat with changes to Earth's climate. The front where the ice contacts the sea bottom pushes up long ridges. With each retreat, a new one of these ridges is left on the sea floor. Later advances by the glacier tend to seal against the old ridges, thus preventing warm seawater from getting under the ice shelf. The ridges therefore retard the melting of the glacier. It was this relationship between the bottom of the ice shelf, the sea floor, the water salinity, and the precise warmth of the sea that Fishy was now documenting. Fine changes could cause major melting at the ice front.

As Fishy made its run, it gave out occasional strobes of bright light. These allowed sufficient photography work without an overly heavy drain on the batteries. In one short sequence, a leopard seal swam down to have a look. It soon decided that Fishy was not good to eat and left.

The bottom was covered with a carpet of life. Brittle stars were the most common, with their spindly arms that waved slowly about. Nothing moved quickly. Some of the fish were as clear as glass and were known to have antifreeze in their blood.

Canyon

Fishy swam a grid pattern, changed depth, and repeated it. It was building up a great cube of data. That grid crossed over a large ridge that was shown grounding the ice shelf in the last survey, but now Fishy could swim clear.   The heat of the ocean was creeping even farther up Thwaites' canyon.

If the glacier had not been there, nor the sea, then what would be there was a canyon much bigger and deeper than the Grand Canyon. This canyon defined one edge of the Trans-Antarctic mountain range. If the ice was not filling that canyon, then enormous amounts of ice would flow through the valleys in those mountains and end up in the sea. It would mean the end of most coastal cities from the resulting sea level rise of several meters this century.

Would this rise happen? Would it take decades or millennia? The key was the heat at this precise location at the transition from sea to ice. Fishy's focus was on finding out the ground truth of this question and finding out right there, right now.

Recovery

Fishy finished a layer of his matric, checked his battery, and then checked the elapsed time. This swim was almost over. It turned back somewhat sadly toward the open sea following the path it had come in.

A few hours later, it broke surface in an open patch well away from the glacier front. It fired up its beacons and its satellite link. This near to either pole, all the sun-sync satellites converge. There would be many overhead passes available very soon.

Fishy did not have to wait long. First, the *David Attenborough* responded to its beacon, and then a satellite pass allowed Fishy to upload fourteen minutes of data. It was to stay where it was and to expect the ship before dark on this long day, and well before bad weather could set in.

Sarah and JanetA were at the rail again when the *David Attenborough* made a slow pass beside Fishy and then positioned for the recovery. Sarah saw now that she had been talking to the wrong AI.

"You remember the little talk we had about the sea talking to me?" said Sarah.

"Certainly, but seas still don't talk," insisted JanetA.

"I will find someone else to talk with," said Sarah. "You are off the hook for now."

That imagined conversation would have to wait until Fishy-Fishy-Fishface14 was safely recovered, and its full data set downloaded. There would be plenty of time once Fishy was latched back in its traveling frame. It would be a long voyage home, plenty of time for a talk.

Did JanetA need to be there for that conversation? No, not at all.

Sometimes even being a good symbiont meant preserving your personal space and your right to have private conversations.

~~~***~~~

[End]
~~~